Black Pearls

Black Pearls

A Faerie Strand

by Louise Hawes

illustrations by Rebecca Guay

Houghton Mifflin Company
Boston 2008

www.houghtonmifflinbooks.com

The text of this book is set in AT Hadriano Light with Norlik Ital.
The illustrations were created with graphite and paint and digitally enhanced.

Library of Congress Cataloging-in-Publication
Hawes, Louise.
Black pearls : a faerie strand / by Louise Hawes ; illustrations by Rebecca Guay.
v. cm.
Contents: Dame Nigran's tower—Pipe dreams—Mother love—
Ashes—Evelyn's song—Diamonda—Naked.
ISBN-13: 978-0-618-74797-9
1. Fairy tales—United States. 2. Children's stories, American. [1. Fairy tales.
2. Short stories.] I. Guay-Mitchell, Rebecca, ill. II. Title.
PZ8.H3126Bl 2008
[Fic]—dc22
2007041166

Manufactured in the United States of America
QUM 10 9 8 7 6 5 4 3 2 1

*This book is dedicated with love to
Regan and Stephen.*

Black Pearls

Contents

Dame Nigran's Tower

*F*lying had come naturally to her. When she'd grown of age and joined the ceremony in the grove, Tabbatha Nigran found her body lifting even before the words were done. She had lost herself and the others each time she'd spun into the night, turning like a thistle, up and up. There were no words for what she felt then, nor did she try to find them. It was simply the reason she lived, the place she had to go, the answer to every question she would ever ask.

> *Daughters of the Moon,*
> *children of the Night,*
> *rise like dew together*
> *until the morning's light.*

When Tabby chanted with her companions, she could scarcely sort her voice from theirs. The song was like a braid, binding them together, joining them in the sacred rite:

> *The owl's cry is our anthem,*
> *our altar is the sky.*

*The Great Mystery is our Mother
to whom now, sisters, fly.*

Held fast in the wind's strong arms, tumbling through the lacy mists of clouds, Tabby seldom gave a thought to landing, only let her heart swell like the moon, only set her face to the west, where she fancied the sun lay in its dark bed. Landing always came too soon on those magic nights. And it always stung. Not in a physical sense, of course. For it was not the actual coming down—the crisp, almost smug way her toes found the ground—that bothered Tabby. It was the return to earth and to the small minds and shriveled hearts that waited for her there: to the pack of dogs that chased her when she left the house, and to the filthy, rheumy children who parroted singsong rhymes—"Witch, witch, fell in a ditch, set her hair on fire."

Tabby never thought of herself as a witch, nor had her adoptive sisters ever used the word. They called themselves Wise Women, and she knew no way but theirs. The coven had taken her in as a babe, had given her love and a home and the sweet, wild joy of flight. That joy, they told her, was neither sorcery nor heritage. It was the gift of every woman who comes to her first blood when the moon is full.

She left the coven before her seventeenth summer and found a place as a weaver's apprentice. When the old woman died, Tabby stayed on in her teacher's humble cottage, but her neighbors could not forget where she'd been raised. No women brought her handiwork and no men came courting.

Tabby knew better than to try to change things. She kept to herself instead, tending the lush garden behind her cottage gate. Everything there brought her solace: the peonies, their great heads crisscrossed by delirious ants; the four o'clocks, slow to wake but glorious till dawn; the sweetpeas and primroses, unruly as children. Even the kitchen plants filled her with pride when she tended them mornings, her hands diving like pale fish among their leaves.

The villagers called her "hellcat" and "twisted faerie" or sometimes "devil's handmaid." But her snapdragons only nodded at her, blushing in the early sun. Through her garden wall, behind the tumbled ivy, Tabby heard her neighbors gossip: "'Tis said she flies at night . . . By God's blood, the milk she begged from me turned sour as I set it at her door . . . Old witches must be young ones first, you know. Have you marked how she leaves her house when'er the Sabbath falls on full moon?"

But her baby roses told no tales, only stared at her shyly from their green nests. So Dame Tabbatha Nigran kept her own counsel. She suffered the town's talk with patience and a resignation born of practice—years of it. She had her flowers and few regrets. Still, there were times, in the green quiet of her garden, when she wondered what it might have been like to have a family and a mother. Instead of sitting, when she was small, in the middle of the dream circle, lifted by dozens of arms as the drowsiness of their spells overtook her, what if she had been cradled in someone's lap? Tabby had seen mothers in town, tending their babes. She had even heard, one night as she made her way across Old

Chauncey's field to the woods, her neighbor singing an off-key lullaby to her youngest. Tabby had peered through the window of the cottage, then, and seen the two of them beside the hearth.

There was something in the way Dame Chauncey held that little one, in the way her voice purred and cracked with tenderness. The scene had lodged itself in Tabby's mind or heart, she was never sure which. Like a tune she didn't know the words to, or a person she could not name, the picture came back to her again and again.

She blamed that picture for what happened the following autumn, when the bearded fellow scaled her garden wall. She had found him knee-deep in the watercress and rampion. The bells were silent and all the town dark, and yet there he was, bending over her plants, tearing them up by the fistful.

"And what be your business in a poor woman's garden?" She'd come up behind him, surprising him quite as much, she noticed with satisfaction, as the sight of him had startled her.

When he stood up, the moonlight turned his hair to ink, made his face look white and sickly. He had spilled some of the greens and was stuffing the rest down his vest. He was a long, large-boned man, but Tabby had seldom seen anyone so frightened. "Forgive me, good madam," he stammered, stooping to retrieve the cap he had let fall. "I only meant . . . That is, I was just . . . If you would be so kind . . ."

Tabby liked the look of his face, blanched with fear, his eyes glassy currants. She was ashamed of the pride that shot through her, knowing she was the cause of his stammer and his clumsi-

ness, of his high, pinched voice. Awkward with this uncommon upper hand, she said the first thing she could think of to keep him scared: "There will be a price, you know."

The fellow looked behind him then, as if he were considering running right through the stone wall he had just climbed. When he turned back, his voice broke and tears shone in the corners of his currant eyes. "Please, my lady," he said. "I means only to put by for my family."

Tabby leaned close, touching his wrist. "A thief's rampion," she told him, "comes dearer than an honest man's." She wondered who he was, this intruder. She knew he was not Elsbeth Chauncey's husband, nor the son of the widow who sold Tabby milk. As for other men in the village, she had seen only the tinker and the market-day vendors. This fellow had not been among them.

The stranger bowed now, and bowed again. "Anything, madam," he said, clutching his cap. "The greens is for my wife, madam. She is with child and craves them fierce."

"So fierce you could not wait until morning and knock on my door?" As Tabby bent to pick up the scattered leaves, the nervous thief pulled back from her. What tales had he heard? What visions danced in his head? "So fierce you need take what is not your own?"

"Ah!" He'd kept twisting his cap as if it were wringing wet, kneading and smoothing it against his chest. "Alas!" His eyes looked to the heavens, begging the wafer moon instead of her, "Please, madam, have mercy on a poor soul who meant no harm."

Still contrary, still perversely glad to see him in such discomfort, Tabby waved her hand at the dark tangle of garden. "There is a stone knocked from my wall," she scolded. "And just look how you have trampled my beds."

"But surely, lady," the man had pleaded, "even such as yourself must feel for the unborn babe my wife carries." Mistaking Tabby's stunned silence for compassion, he pressed on. "Even a fiend would not deprive an innocent babe of its father."

"If you have fathered innocence," Tabby told him, recovering, "where, pray tell, is the guilty party?"

"God preserve us, there be none, madam. 'Twas the mindless craving of a woman with child, is all. 'John, I must have rampion or die,' she tells me. Those be her very words."

"Indeed?" Tabby fixed her eyes on his. "She said, '*die*'?" If he wanted a witch, she would give him one. "She meant to *die* for her supper?"

"No! No! You shall not take her life! Here!" He pulled the leaves from his vest and forced them into Tabby's hands. "I will take no more plants, nary a one. On my own head, last night was the end. I swear."

"Last night?" Tabby felt a tingle, a shiver of power. "You have been here before?"

"Oh, Lord! Oh, saints above!" The man dropped to his knees, grabbed the hem of her skirt. "I will do anything, give you all I have. Only spare my wife."

Tabby had not answered, wondering what service she could

exact from this man. If he was as strong as he looked, there was a shed to be built and hay to be brought in before frost.

"You can have the babe." He stood suddenly, as if they had just come to terms. "I know that be what you crave, an innocent soul to turn to devil's work."

"Listen, fellow." Tabby was almost amused by the picture he nursed in his brain—a child-snatching witch, an unnatural hag who could not give birth and so must steal others' babes. "I ask only some honest labor in return for what you have taken from me."

"Ay, and when the child is grown, ye shall have it," the man told her. He placed his cap again on his head and bowed to Tabby, moving backward all the while. "A sturdy lad or lass to fetch and carry."

"Do you honestly expect me to wait years for what is owed me?" Why did she not laugh? Why did she not mention the shed or the hay, the wood that needed splitting?

"You be fouler than you seem, dame." His eyes found hers, and he resumed his pitiable handwringing. "A black heart in a fair frame."

It was time she set the fool straight. Tabby followed him and again touched his wrist. "Listen, my good man," she said. "I shall—"

"Yes! Yes! You shall have the babe as soon as it is weaned, I will bring it to you. On my oath."

"Weaned?"

"Ay, madam. As the Savior is my witness, the babe is yours."

He stopped his scuttling crab walk and uttered a single bleating sob. "But it is a human child. It must suck at its mother's teat."

"But I do not want—"

He held his arms in front of him, as if to fend her off. "Ye have my oath, I say. Only do not harm my wife and me." Now that he had reached the gate he turned and, like some frantic animal, tried to walk through it without lifting the latch. At last he remembered himself and, making small, panicked grunts, succeeded in lifting the lock and racing off into the night.

A baby! Tabby had hardly dared hope for such a thing. Nor did she let herself dwell on the thought for long after the man left. Her satisfaction at having frightened him, in fact, soon gave way to self-recrimination: A fine witch, she was! Why, she had not even thought to ask his name or where he came from. Even now, he must be laughing at how he'd outsmarted her. She would surely never see him again.

It was not until spring, when buds shouldered their way once more out of the earth, that she allowed herself to think of the promise. She pictured a child, curled like a shoot in its mother's belly, and wondered idly how it was that someone went about being a parent. What did you feed them? And how did you hold one without hurting it? Not that the answers mattered, she scolded herself. Not that they mattered at all. Best to set aside such foolishness and put the new spade she'd bought at market to work. Radishes needed to be sown deep.

So if you had asked her, Tabby would have said she was not ex-
pecting it, did not want it at all. But when the man came back
the next fall, carrying the girl in his arms, her eyes had filled with
tears of relief. She could not speak, but drank up the child with
a thirsty heart: already pretty, the tiny thing had yellow curls
and eyes as blue as the irises that grew in a thick, companionable
cluster by Tabby's well. But it was not the dainty features or fair
hair that stunned her, that flooded her own face with warmth.
It was the way the baby leaned from her father's hold and
reached her arms toward Tabby, as if she meant to fly across the
space between them.

Though Tabby was speechless, the man was a veritable gossip. His wife was pregnant again, he told her, and though he
hated to part with his firstborn, he knew, fiend that she was,
Tabby would hex the second babe if he did not. This one was
weaned and walking, and a stout little soul besides. Her needs
were few, and she looked as though she would grow into a
strong worker. But four were a lot of mouths to feed, and if the
new child was a son, why, he bore no grudge. Even witches
could be made to serve God's plan.

Tabby said nothing, only stared at the treasure he carried.

"Farewell, my Rampion, my tender babe," he told his daughter at last, setting her down and striding to the door. "God keep
you in his care." He stepped outside and without another word
left the child standing in front of the hearth. He did not look
back or wave to the babe he had named after a kitchen green, but
hurried off as if Tabby might change her mind.

The girl did not look after him, only studied Tabby solemnly, then climbed onto her lap and fell asleep. Tabby had wanted to run after the man, to find out where he lived, to ask the count-less questions that suddenly occurred to her. She needed clothes for the child, and shoes, and toys. She wondered if Rampion had ever been sick or whether there were foods she must not have. But the weight of that small creature kept her pinned to her chair, fearful of talking or moving lest the moment dissolve like a bubble in a stream.

Rampion. A strange name, but a good one, Tabby thought. Some girls were called Rose, after all, and some Violet or Pansy or Blossom. Wasn't it better to bear the name of a sturdy little plant, a green that flowered in the summer and gave food the rest of the year? As she listened to the shallow, even breaths of the babe in her lap, she closed her eyes and tried to feel her way through the years that lay ahead. Tabby was not blessed, as some in the coven were, with the gift of second sight, so the image she saw was more yearning than certainty, but it was a comfort nonetheless— a girl fair enough to be a princess, with a slender, graceful form and a laugh that tumbled like falls down a mossy bank.

She did not know how long they sat, the little one curled against her with her left thumb in her mouth, Tabby rigid with bliss, counting the small heartbeats that drummed against her own chest. But when Rampion finally stirred, her father was long gone and it was too late to ask him anything at all. They must make do, the two of them, with just each other.

And make do, they did. Though she could speak only baby

nonsense, Tabby's new daughter (daughter! the word was too sweet to say aloud) made her wants clear. And each one was given her, nearly as soon as she pointed or cried or smiled at it.

Tabby hugged and fed and petted and played. She sang and clapped and laughed and jigged. She made dolls from old bed sheets and crowns from dried periwinkle and sweet William. By spring, the girl had spoken her first words, and by late summer, she was chattering like a magpie, telling her rag dolls secrets or begging her mother for treats. Though Tabby fell into bed each night panting with exhaustion, she lay sleepless for hours, tense and hopeful, her love like a hunger that could only be fed by Rampion's waking and wanting more.

She let the garden go to seed. All except the vegetables and herbs she grew to feed the child. There were not enough hours in the day to waste on primroses. Tabby was tending something far more precious now—something that responded to her care by growing more beautiful with every season. There were times, often when she sat stitching, that she looked up to find the girl playing in a stripe of sunlight spread across the floor. She would stop then, losing a stitch she would have to pick up later, and stare at the fearful loveliness of her daughter. And when, feeling doting eyes on her, Rampion looked up as well, she would likely run and put her arms around Tabby's neck, settle in her lap, and set to unpinning her own bright curls. "Mother! Mother!" she would beg. "Brush my hair."

Then Tabby would stroke Rampion's shining locks with a brush she had bought at market, a fine one made of willow wood and boar's bristles. The soft lapping of the brush, the hair falling pale as light across her daughter's shoulders, it worked the same miracle every time—the soaring inside her chest, her heart straining up and up. Her body never left the chair, but her mind and spirit flew away to the sweet future when her lovely child would grow to womanhood, when Tabby would take her by the hand to the sacred grove. When she would teach her what she knew of splendor, of endless joy.

Because she cherished this vision, the two of them flying together, Tabby's garden died before her meetings with the coven stopped. But it was not long after the peonies withered, their wilted heads drooping on broken stalks, that Tabby began to find reasons to miss the gatherings with her sisters in the woods. What had been her greatest joy was now cheating her of one far greater. Each time she left her daughter, she suffered dreadfully, imagining an endless variety of accidents and illnesses that might strike while Rampion was alone. What if the girl were to wake feeling thirsty, for instance? Were to push a stool against the wall to reach the cupboard overhead? And what if the stool tipped and sent her sprawling? Or say she managed to lift the latch and wander outside while Tabby was away? There were snakes in the old garden wall; Tabby had seen them several times at dusk, slithering out of sight before she could find their nest. The night she remembered this, Tabby tortured herself with a vision of

Rampion being bitten, falling to the ground, then crying for her mother, calling and calling until she had no breath left but lay still and cold.

When Tabby finally told them she could no longer come to the woods, the others had been sad but not surprised. "You have caught the way of human love," her friend Maeve warned her. "'Tis not a bad way, but it clouds the heart and will make you weak. The Great Mother will ne'er abandon you, but 'tis you that will draw away from her. Further and further, until you have forgotten how to fly."

Tabby had laughed, knowing she would always remember the upward thrust, the whirling through moonlit air. "'Twill not be for long," she reminded them all. "Only until my daughter"—she said it out loud now, proudly—"comes of age. We will return to these woods after her first blood. The two of us."

Maeve and the others had nodded, but it was clear they did not believe her. "Paths are never straight," Sheba said, pointing the same finger at Tabby she had once used to show her the stars in the sky. "Turnings and choices leave tangles behind."

Tabby's old teacher drew her close. "You are not likely to find your way back to us." She kissed the younger woman, but it was a sad kiss, one that Tabby felt for a long time on her cheek, like a print, a seal of farewell.

After that night, she did not meet with the others again. Though she sometimes felt the urge to fly alone, to shoot like a lance through the dark, she stayed true to her changed life and

her new responsibilities. These last were so consuming that they kept her from self-pity. Rampion was soon old enough for lessons. Tabby could not teach her to embroider or play the spinet like the daughter of the village mayor, but she had her own skills to pass on. The kitchen garden was still intact, and if Tabby had not raised the stone wall until it met the bottom branches of her cherry tree, their neighbors might have seen the two of them gathering herbs each morning, might have stopped to listen to Rampion's cheerful recitation: "Burdock for skin and blood; goldenseal for what ails; yarrow for strength, and . . ." Sometimes she would break off, forgetting the name of a plant. "What is this one, Mother? It has an awful stink! I hope 'twill vanish in the stew!"

"'Tis tansy, love," Tabby told her, smiling at the way the girl's lips and nose had nearly met in the center of her darling face. "The root for fevers and flies, the leaves for puddings and cakes."

"Then let us leave the root in the ground," Rampion had decided. "'Twill grow more leaves that way, and you know how I love pudding!"

There were cooking lessons, too. And darning. And the smattering of Latin Tabby had learned from the coven. It was mostly words that went with flying spells, not the church Latin the other children in town knew. Her sisters' church, after all, had been the wild woods, and their prayers had focused on thanksgiving, not penance, on the Great Mother, not the Holy Father. So it was little wonder that, at last, Rampion came to be regarded with the same suspicion and fear her mother was.

It did not happen all at once. There were only whispers at first, some nervous laughter when Tabby and her daughter appeared in public. But if Rampion chanced to stretch her tiny arm toward a stranger and utter a Latin phrase she had learned, some mistook it for an incantation. And once when they had gone to a fair in Bridley and Rampion tried to join a group of children watching a Punch and Judy show, the other children's mothers, one by one, had pulled their sons and daughters away from the stage. But in those early years, while Rampion was still a child, the two managed to brush shoulders with the rest of the village, and no great harm was done on either side. In fact, Tabby began to enjoy taking the girl with her to market, loved the way Rampion's cheeks reddened with the fresh air, the way people stared at her loveliness. Sometimes the tradesmen and shoppers even made timid overtures, handing the child sweets and trinkets or stroking her hair and asking if fairies had spun it. It made the final blow all the more cruel, then, that it came on market day.

It happened when Rampion was eleven years old, when her beauty had already begun to stop people in their tracks, to make them gossip and whisper things that sat like stones in Tabby's chest: Was such a face normal? Were Christ's children meant to be so alluring? Did her sweet shape dissolve at night, turn into the scab-infested leer and hairy chest of devil's spawn?

Perhaps if the hurt had traveled no further than her own anxious love, Tabby would not have run away, would not have packed up her daughter and taken to the forest like a gypsy. But one day when Rampion joined two girls playing at hoops in the

market square, a group of older boys surrounded her. Tabby was bargaining with the apple woman when the boys' song made her turn:

> *Witch's Child, you cannot cry*
> *when I pinch you low or high.*
> *Fie! Fie! Four fingers round my thumb!*
> *You must not walk where good folk come.*

Though Rampion eventually forgot the teasing, Tabby relived the ugly scene for weeks on end. It was still buried like a barb in her heart the day she packed their belongings and set off toward an old tower she had found in the woods. "They shall ne'er treat you like that again," she told the girl. Just as she had at market, Rampion sobbed piteously. But this time it was Tabby, and not the village bullies, who made her weep. She held fast to her mother's skirts and did all she could to prevent her from stuffing the last of the cookware into two bulging saddlebags on the hollow-flanked mare they had borrowed from Old Chauncey.

"It does not matter," the girl insisted, pursuing her mother into the forest and stumbling along the nearly invisible path Tabby seemed to find without effort. "For my sake, Mother, let it be. I would rather get teased every day than leave our lovely garden."

But Tabby could not forget how the children had poked and prodded, trying to prove a witch cannot cry—"*. . . when I pinch you low or high.*" How each had wrapped one fist around his other

thumb and pummeled Rampion with both hands joined. Even when the girl began to sob, they did not stop, and afterward her slender arms had been riddled with ugly scratches and bruises.

The tower did little to comfort Rampion, though the shock of it stopped her tears. Jutting from the undergrowth at a slight angle, it no longer belonged to a castle but stood by itself, a crumbling ruin pointing halfheartedly at the sky. Even Tabby was dispirited as they neared the place, wondering if it could ever be made habitable. She heard the need to please in her own voice, the desperate enthusiasm. "See, love, there's a window on high," she told her daughter. "You shall be mistress of all you survey."

The girl sniffed and looked up to where two stone gargoyles guarded the tower's single window. "Then I will be mistress of fearsome rocks and noisome weeds." She kicked aside a clump of mandrake that barred her way and tied their mule to a tree. Pulling an ax from a satchel on its back, she called over her shoulder, "Come along, Mother. It would seem we must work until last light to part our front door from these woods."

It was true. What once must have been a guard's entrance was all but swallowed up by thick, gnarled vines and brambles. After they had chopped away the brush and forced the small door open, they found a stairway that was sound enough to climb. They followed it to the top of the tower, a spacious, high-walled room brightened on one side by the window and on the other by a second, larger door. Years before, Tabby supposed, this entrance might have opened into the castle. But if anyone had

been foolish enough to walk through it now, they would have found no footing, only dropped like a stone to the woods below.

That first day and many after, Tabby and the girl scrubbed and polished. They hauled bedding, benches, and trestles from the house they had left behind and dragged them up the winding stairs. For though they placed a few sconces and a braided rug in the hall on the ground floor, most of their belongings had to be carried to the topmost room, where the window and the old door-way let in a comforting, buttery light. They pushed a chest against the larger opening and hung thick curtains, turning it into a pass-able window. Through a chink that Tabby assumed had once served to rain arrows on soldiers below, they vented a hearth.

At last, even Rampion had to admit, they had fashioned an elegant aerie. Whereas the old cottage had made their posses-sions seem dingy and small, the high stone walls of the tower lent everything they owned a sort of spare majesty. "I shall be quite afraid to sing at baking here," Tabby told her daughter. "It seems more fit for curtsies and perfumed handkerchiefs, this grand place we have made!"

"On the contrary, Mother." Rampion, who had not smiled in days, laughed and put down her broom. "'Tis made for trills and long, sweet notes." She picked up her skirts, then whirled around the huge room, singing as she spun. The combination of her daughter's tender form and the wild gaiety in her voice made Tabby stop work, dizzy with love, to lean against her own broom.

All went well for a few months. Rampion spent hours watching the woods and the fields beyond from the tower window. And when she tired of looking at the land below them, she spent even more hours tramping through the forest outside their door. Tabby's fear of people made her trust the places where they were not. She never worried about her daughter, who came home from these walks with herbs and flowers and mushrooms; with baskets of acorns, blackberries, and the tiny, ripe fruits they christened "wood plums."

What the wild world did not provide, Tabby secured by hard work. If Rampion begged for a new gown, her mother would hire herself out as a servant in town until it was bought. If the girl wanted a book, a few more weeks of work and Tabby could place it in her lap. And if the book was opened to a picture of a beautiful dame in a necklace for which Rampion pined, sure enough, Tabbatha Nigran overcame her hatred of the village folk long enough to clean their houses and wash their filthy linens. As she worked, she dreamed only of the moment she could fasten those flashing gems around her daughter's neck.

When she did, the girl's rapturous smile was worth every ache in Tabby's back, every morning spent on stiff knees. "Oh!" Rampion stared at her reflection in the looking glass they had bought at Bridley the year before. "It is the loveliest thing I have ever seen!" She watched the play of light on her new necklace, staring as if spelled into the glass. "Will you brush my hair the way you used to, Mother? I feel as though I am quite outshined!"

Rampion unpinned her hair, and Tabby was astonished to see

how long it had grown. Reaching past her ankles, it rolled across the floor in frothy golden waves. The bristle brush was found and Tabby sat in the light from the window while, weak with fondness, she worked through the tangled locks, down and down.

The evening Tabby found the upside-down cross nailed to their door, she did not tell Rampion. She had come home late from serving at a burgher's saint's day feast and was so tired, she failed to notice the two branches tied together and fastened just above eye level. It was the smell of the blood splashed across them that made her stop, made her draw back and cover her nose. Once she had tiptoed upstairs and seen that her daughter still slept, she snuck back down the stairs again, tore away the hateful token, and cleaned the door until no trace remained.

Tabby was well aware that she courted such hate by working in town, but she had hoped it would not find their woodland home. Now the sign of the witch had been tacked to their door. *We know where you are,* it seemed to say. *We will not let you rest.* Next morning, she took the padlock from her chest upstairs and fastened it on the little door.

"You shall not leave the house today, my pet." She tried to keep the worry from her tone, worked not to sound too sharp or stern. "For a while, you must wait until I come home to go a'rambling." The day at the fair threatened to play itself out again in her mind, and she shook her head to banish the ugly scene. "And you must not go too far, must never stray toward town."

"But why?" Rampion was accustomed to being on her own in the forest, to tramping when and where she pleased.

"I will tell you by and by, but for now you shall do as I say." Tabby softened, melted by the girl's anguished expression. "Have I ere wanted more than your safety and content?"

The first few days were hard, since no matter how early Tabby rushed home to unlock the tower door, it was never soon enough. "The sun is nearly down," the girl would moan. "I shall have no time at all." Or, "Mother!" she would cry. "You have caged me like a beast!"

But then, for no reason Tabby could find, things settled into an easier pattern. Rampion was sweeter now, always ready with soup and a smile when her mother came home and unlocked the door. Occasionally, she even chose to stay inside rather than take to the woods. "The forest will be there tomorrow," she would say, making Tabby's grateful heart leap. "But you are tired, Mother, and will soon to bed. If we are to sing and sew a bit, we'd best be about it now."

In this way the winter turned to spring, and Rampion asked only a few times when her imprisonment would end. She was easily put off with Tabby's assurances that it would be soon, and indeed, the cross on the tower door began to seem a mere prank, the idle threat of a child. So when, on the first day of a full moon in April, Tabby's dreams came true at last, there was nothing to dilute her joy. "Mother," the girl announced over their mugs of

morning porridge, "I must have cut myself on my walk last night. Look how I have spoiled my gown." As soon as she saw the red nightshirt, Tabby's eyes filled. *First blood,* she thought. *My daughter is a woman made for flight.*

She embraced Rampion and explained that the blood was a ripeness, not a wound. She showed her how to bind herself, how to wash the cloth and bind again. "And when the blood has stopped," she promised, barely containing her joy, "and the moon is new again, we will take to the woods, you and I." She drew the girl to the window they had fashioned of the useless door, and together they looked out at the forest below. "I will show you a secret there, a secret only we two can share." She pictured the clearing in the woods, imagined them joining the coven's flight. Already, as if it had been days instead of years, she could feel the swift climb, the unstoppable cresting, like a tide in her veins.

The next day, instead of heading for the village, Tabby hurried to the sacred grove. Or rather, to the spot she was convinced she had visited so often before. But when she reached the clearing, she found the ground overgrown with weeds and the altar of stones missing. There were no stray boulders, no tumbled remains at all. It was as if she and her sisters had never met, had never chanted the sacred words or worn the earth smooth with their comings and goings. Could she have forgotten the path? How could her feet have failed to take her the way she knew as well as she knew her name?

For a while she stood, head bent, silent. It was almost like disappearing, losing the last traces of her past this way. But

when she looked up again, she was still herself, still the mother of the dearest, fairest child she could imagine. She had not, after all, heard from her sisters in years, had not sought them out or missed them more than a handful of times. Those nights, when the moon swelled and the time of flight neared, she had dreamt of going with them, had felt awash with the old yearning, the call to the sky. But such dreams vanished like dew in the morning, burned away in the fierce love she knew would outlast all others. Nor did she need the sisterhood, she decided now, to pass on the glorious rite, to fly with Rampion at the very next full moon.

As she made her way home, it occurred to Tabby that the coven might simply have grown old. She herself, after all, had been the youngest of them, and the rest (she felt suddenly guilty at the thought) might have died. Part of her grieved her lost friends, while another part trembled with eagerness to share the sweetest secret she knew with Rampion. Little wonder, then, that she failed to notice the second bloody tribute until it met her eye to eye. No harmless cross of twigs this time: it was a goat's head that had been hacked off and nailed to their tower door. The dead eyes were wide, as if stunned by the loss of the body they had been accustomed to steering. The tongue lolled, and a steady red stream still poured from the severed neck. Tabby's first thought was *Poor thing.* Her second was *We must run.*

She realized now that the coven had probably left long before, driven out by the same hatred and violent fear that had turned

the village against Tabby and her daughter. There was no time to lose, she told Rampion as soon as she had unlocked the door and hurried upstairs; they must escape right away. "I cannot leave you alone again," she said. "I dare not trust your safety, even in our own home."

"And where, pray tell, will we go?" Rampion clearly feared the unknown more than the threats of bullies, which were, after all, quite familiar to her. "They mean nothing, those louts," she told Tabby. "They box with shadows and call themselves men. When I go to town, I point a finger at them and they all fall back, hexed. "

"When you go to town?" Tabby was stunned. And furious.

Rampion blushed. "Only once in a while," she said, "when I have finished picking . . ." She stopped, shamed by the look on her mother's face.

"I have told you not to walk beyond the woods, have I not?"

"Dear old worrywart!" Rampion smiled fondly at Tabby now. "I ne'er go far. Only to meet my friend for a walk or a game. Or sometimes to peek at the market stalls."

"Friend?" Tabby's hand was on her throat as she sat heavily, suddenly. "What friend, daughter?"

"There, there." The girl touched Tabby's arm as if she were settling a nervous horse. "Do not be peevish. 'Tis only for fun now and then." She hoisted her skirt to show her pretty foot. "Surely you do not mean me to hide the lovely frocks you buy me? Must no one see my finery?" She turned this way and that, jigging

steps she could not have taught herself. "There are those in town who fancy my company, Mother, who wait for me to come."

Tabby hid her eyes from her daughter's spinning dance, from the mischief in her smile. She felt little curiosity about her daughter's companions, only the need, savage and certain, to banish them from the girl's life. "You shall not cross me on this, my Rampion. I will make you safe until I find a refuge for us, a new home far from such friends as nail a goat head to your door."

Rampion stopped her dance and bent to put a patient hand on Tabby's knee. "I know no one who would do such a thing, Mother. And a new home will be no refuge for me." She stood straight again, surveyed the dark forest outside the window. "I need to sing and dance. I need to see my friend."

Tabby was certain the girl meant no harm. It seemed to her that Rampion must have snuck into town with the same careless innocence that sometimes made her bring home the wrong mushrooms, the ones that might have killed them both. She was young, after all, and could not know the deadly poisons stored in human hearts. So Tabby struck a bargain, made a promise she hoped would save them both: "I will show you, Rampion my own," she told the girl, "such freedom as you ne'er could dream. Give me until the open moon, and stay inside until the first night she turns her white face on us." It was not so much to ask, surely, of the child she had fed and raised and loved until she felt her heart might burst. "Then, when you have seen what I will share, if you do not want to come away with me, we will stay here." Once her daughter had felt the night sky against her face,

Tabby knew, once she had sifted moonlight between her outstretched fingers, she could never prefer the tame pleasures of flightless companions.

"But when you come home, surely then I can go out?"

"No, pet," Tabby told her. "We must take no chances until I have earned enough to give us a fresh start in a town with kinder folk." She held her daughter's hands, like two trapped birds, between her own. "But I will bring you dainties and games each night. 'Twill make the next day pass so quickly, you will swear the sun has mistaken its course."

To Tabby's surprise, though she sighed a bit and pouted mightily, Rampion agreed. She did not weep or complain of being held captive but settled with a good will beside her mother, taking up her needle. "'Tis but two fortnights," she said, sounding almost cheerful. "I will sew some new sleeves for your gown to keep myself busy. And stir the pot till you come home."

Though she should have been relieved, Tabby slept poorly that night. She dreamt of the goat she had found on the door—not just its head, but the whole goat, swelled to giant size. Its beard was as big as a tree and its hooves sparked lightning as it ran. It lowered its shaggy head and stormed toward the tower, snorting like a bull. Desperate to save Rampion, who she knew was inside, Tabby began to build a wall across the tower door. Just as she had fashioned the wall around her old garden, she laid stone on top of stone in her dream, building higher and higher. But as she put each stone in place, she saw the goat-bull coming closer, felt the earth shudder under its flashing hooves. Just as

she was tapping the last stone into place, she heard a hideous roar and woke from the nightmare, her pallet tumbled off its platform and her nightshirt soaked with sweat.

The dream stayed with her all the next day, so that instead of going into town to work, Tabby went back to the cottage where she had raised Rampion. She was glad the girl was not with her to see what had become of their little home. Marked with an inverted cross like the one that had been tacked on the tower, its shutters burnt away and its door gaping wide, the house had been plundered until it was little more than a pile of rotting timbers. But the round stones in the wall suited Tabby's purpose, and by twos and threes she succeeded at last in hauling several score back to the tower in the woods. The next day, with wet earth and sand for mortar, she managed to seal up the tower door just as she had done in her dream.

It was cruel, backbreaking work, but even though Rampion begged to come down and help, Tabby was too caught up in her dream and her fears to let the girl out. Stone by heavy stone, she covered up the door and barely paid attention when her daughter leaned from the window to tease her. "For all you love me, Mother, this old monster is luckier far than I." She reached down to touch the tongue of one of the gargoyles that perched below the window ledge. "For here he sits in the sweet open air, while I am forced to sniff last night's fire and yesterday's soup."

So intent was Tabby on her labors that she neither smiled at her daughter's antics nor gave a thought to how she herself would enter and leave the place until the moon was full and the

power of flight was strong in her again. Only after she had set the last stone and smelled the lentils Rampion put on to cook did she remember the end of her dream, the horror of finding herself on the wrong side of the wall. But this, of course, was different. There was no nightmarish beast storming toward Tabby now, only the foolish shame of having sealed herself away from her daughter and deprived herself of her own bed!

Mortified and bone weary, she was far too exhausted to laugh at her mistake. Instead, daunted and tired beyond measure, she sat down by the vanished door and wept. With no room for pride, she sobbed so long and hard that Rampion, who had never before seen Tabby cry, was moved to tears herself. "Please, Mother," she called from the window. "Please do not despair. We will solve this riddle by and by." And it was not long at all before she did.

Tabby wiped her eyes and stared in astonishment when her clever girl showed how she could twist her long hair into a braid and wrap it around the open jaw of one of the gargoyles. When she had let the braid down as far as it would go, she urged her mother to use it as a rope and climb up. Indeed, once Tabby had obeyed her daughter's instructions and rolled Old Chauncey's cart beneath the window, then clambered on top, she found she could easily grab the lovely, sunny ladder that tumbled down to her and hoist herself home. "'Tis very like flying," she said, pleased and smiling, when she had reached the top.

On the evening of May's full moon—the Milk Moon, the villagers called it—Tabby rushed back to the tower. As she had each day for a month, she called for Rampion to let down her hair. All morning she had nursed her excitement, like something warm nestled against her heart. In a matter of hours, she had told herself as she emptied the villagers' chamber pots and scrubbed their floors, the hunger for flight would come. Rampion must already be feeling the heat in her blood, the stirrings of a woman born to flight.

At first when she called up and heard nothing but the wind whistling through the empty windows, Tabby was not alarmed. "Rampion!" she cried, her hands cupped round her mouth in case the girl was reading or dozing by the fire. "Rampion, let down your hair!" A crow in a tree behind the tower answered, but no yellow braid dropped down to her.

She spent an hour calling and crying, then another seated in a miserable heap beside the walled-up door. As she sat, she remembered how bravely and gaily Rampion had accepted her long imprisonment, and how quickly she had devised the scheme of using her braid to help her mother scale the tower wall. How resourceful and quick she was, this child Tabby had watched grow from a babe in her lap! And how slow and stupid Tabby had been! Why had she not seen it before? She was not the first to have climbed that golden ladder. Rampion must have helped her friend into the tower each day the door was locked and Tabby had the key. How she must have laughed at her mother's

loose and easy love! And now she was gone. Dancing somewhere or laughing with a crowd of friends. Making fun of the simple household hours that were all Tabby ever hoped to know of joy.

Soon she was tearing at the stones with bloody hands, ripping them from the mortar until she'd made a small hole through which she could push open the door. She raced upstairs then and found what she had known she would—an empty room with Rampion's gowns all gone, her trinkets carried off, except for a basket of blackberries placed neatly on the table, and the lovely necklace, which must have come undone and now lay broken, its bright jewels scattered across the floor.

For three days Tabby waited, the hearth untended, sunset and sunrise finding her still beside the window. Sometimes she leaned out to stroke the head of the gargoyle whose gaping mouth had held Rampion's hair. "If witches cry, perhaps monsters can, too," she told the crusty stone. "When she returns, though, we must not tell her how we have wept."

For another week she lived on hope and the few provisions they had stored in the tower. Surely the gift of the berries meant that Rampion cared, that she was coming back. Surely the years of love, and of squabbling, yes, like a hen and her chick, before the two of them settled beside each other, could not have ended.

Finally, though, driven by hunger, Tabby took to the woods to gather wild fruit and to trace her daughter's steps. Each day

she wandered a bit further, fanning out and out from the tower, searching for a small boot print, a dropped handkerchief, a whisper of what she had lost.

Two moons filled, then faded before she heard the tale from gypsies camped in a clearing deep in the woods. It was the story of a witch's child, and the woman who told it to Tabby, juggling two babes on her lap by the fire, had heard it from a groom whose mistress claimed to have learned it from a troubadour who had gotten the tale firsthand from a jester in a palace leagues away.

It seemed an evil witch had won the child from her terrified father and kept her prisoner in a tower. But one day Rapunzel—yes, the woman was certain that was her name—had escaped and run off with a handsome prince. She was a sweet young thing, Rapunzel was, with long flaxen curls, and wasn't it a blessing she had tricked that scheming witch?

"I've heard of such a girl," Tabby told the woman, something inside her crumbling, blowing away like dust. "But her name was Rampion."

"Rampion," the gypsy repeated, her accent heavy, slow. "That is how you say it here, yes?" She held her fingers up to show what she meant. "A small plant for salads, is it not?"

Tabby nodded, desolate.

"In our country, we call it rapunzel." But the gypsy had already forgotten her story. She begged now to trade a beaded belt for the vest Tabby wore. Behind her, her husband proffered a leg of venison to sweeten the deal, but it was all Tabby could do to bid them farewell and stumble back to the tower. There she lit a

fire and threw the girl's necklace into the flames. Then she unclasped a tiny locket from around her neck and took out the strand of yellow hair curled inside. That, too, went into the flames, where it flared, lit up the hearth, and was gone. For a while, as the jewels on the necklace cracked and blackened on the grate, Tabby thought she heard Rampion calling her. "Mother! Mother!" the voice in her head cried until she felt she might go mad. But then, as the gems split apart and finally turned to ash, the voice was quiet at last.

For three days, she slept, dreamless, on her pallet until the light woke her. The moon was full again and calling. Veils of filmy white covered everything in the room, the wind rustled like a woman's gown, and a wood dove mistook the brightness for morning and began to sing. Tabby rose from her bed and pushed the heavy chest from the door. She stared at the indigo woods below her, then turned her gaze to the sky. A fat newborn, the moon drew her to the edge of the doorway, filled her with the old longing.

She leaned out to the night, and the wind nuzzled her bare toes, slipped sly fingers up her gown. She remembered her sisters' warnings. "You have caught the way of human love," Maeve had said. And Tabby had laughed when they told her she would forget how to fly.

Tonight, though, it was not flight she was after. She still knew how to catch an updraft, how to surrender to a current, arms wide. But what Tabby wanted most, what she craved as she stood in the light of her last full moon, was to walk, not fly, from this

door. To leave behind the loneliness that made her days rattle like chains and stole the taste from everything she ate. To drop like a stone and put a stop to the waiting, the mad dream of the girl racing up the tower steps and into her arms. Wasn't such an end better than trying to begin again when a garden was no longer enough? When the sweet, empty face of a flower or the warmth of the sun was nothing beside the rush of air, the final fall?

Pipe Dreams

When the rats ate Herr Bergman's footstool, Father decided to call on the mayor. It was the same day they ate my crutch, but I was the only one who cared about that. The footstool meant money, after all; it was nearly finished and had been left on a workbench near my bed. I had leaned my crutch against the same bench, where it would be within easy reach. Easy reach of the rats, it turned out!

By the time I woke that morning, the footstool had only two legs left and the crutch looked as though a band of beaver had taken a fancy to it. The carved pad on top had been nibbled to a stub, and the rest was nearly four hands shorter than it had been the day before. When I leaned my weight on it, the whole shaft split down the middle and sent me sprawling.

I am not sure which made Father angriest—the sight of me, far too old to be sobbing on the floor in a pile of splinters, or the unpaid hours and new wood it would require to rebuild the stool. I know only that he was red-faced and trembling when he leaned down and yanked me to my feet.

"What will it take?" he yelled, bracing me against him and clamping his huge arm around my waist. "Do those monsters need to eat the trim off his wife's jacket before our fool of a mayor decides to hire the piper?"

I thought of the mayor's wife, a thin woman who walked as if she were standing on her toes inside those fur-lined boots of hers. And then I thought of the egrets I had carved on the top of my crutch, each one carefully polished with mineral spirits until its wings shone.

"A crutch is one thing," Father told me, as if he had heard the words I'd only thought. He steered me toward the workbench, where four small chests waited for finishing. "You can make another in a few hours, if you don't insist on decorating it like an emperor's walking stick." He made a snorting sound, the whinny of a large, steaming horse, then looked forlornly at the mess on the floor.

"This stool was nearly ready." He kicked the legs that remained on the half-chewed base. "The old man will not pay us twice for one stool." He handed me a mallet, unrolled an apron of chisels across the bench, then grabbed his cap and jacket from the pegs by the door. "I will call on the mayor after I fetch the birch," he told me, his tone as stern as if I were the one who had chewed the stool to shreds. "Find what you can for supper, boy. I'll not be back till that lout and his council have come to their senses."

I knew there was endless work ahead. But still I felt slyly grateful, glad that, for once, I was not the "lout" father blamed

for our troubles. Ever since I was four and old enough to hold an awl, father had complained of my work. For nearly eleven years, I had been boxed about the ears and scolded for carving too slowly or polishing too fine. Now, whether or not the members of Hameln's council saw the error of their ways, Father clearly meant to set them straight. Which meant, in turn, that I would spend a whole day without being told that Frau Weedmeir was too blind to notice the finish on her strongbox. Or that unless the young Springmans had turned into royalty overnight, they did not require garlands on their settle.

As the bells of St. Nicolai rang the hour and Father started down the road, it occurred to me that he had misplaced the blame for our woes. It was, after all, that musical rat-chaser, not the council, who was the cause of the infestation. For the piper, it seemed, was entirely too good at his job. Three other towns had already hired him, and now all the vermin he'd sent packing had found their way to Hameln! The slithering rodents were everywhere: in cupboards, where they jumped out if you opened the door; in grain bins, where cooks found their droppings mixed with the chaff; and often as not, in nurseries, where they waited until dark to crawl into the cradles and set the babes howling with their nasty bites.

By the time the bells of St. Bonifatius had begun chiming, too, I was already at work. Not on the jewelry chests Father would expect finished by his return, but on a fresh crutch. Until now I had needed a new one only when I grew too tall for the old. To own the truth, I had been proud each time that happened,

though Father said the only difference between a crippled child and a crippled man was that the man ate more.

Like stragglers trying to catch up, the bells in the church by the river always rang late, so now as those in our cathedral were finishing their song, the latecomers had just begun theirs. Carving as I listened, I was astonished to find my hands deciding on a new design before the rest of me had any inkling what they were about.

I had chosen a small piece of cherry with a sharp, uneven grain that would make it useless in Father's eyes. But it would do for the armrest of my crutch, and as I worked my carving tool along the grain, I created a jagged range of mountains, like the Weserbergland beyond our town. The sky behind the range I left as smooth and empty as a beggar's plate. Yet by the time both bells had fallen silent, I knew what to carve there: just above the mountains I shaped the egrets from my old crutch. Instead of standing on their long legs in a stream, though, these birds soared toward heaven, their wings beating wedge-shaped Vs into the sky. With such wide, beautiful wings, I thought, who needed legs?

When I was born, Mother hid my twisted leg until after the christening. Which is why I was baptized Emmett, a fine old name that means "hard-working and strong." I have proved to be one but not the other, and although Mother used to say "Better a strong heart than a strong back," Father never agreed.

The first thing I remember is learning, much later than most wee ones, to crawl. And the second thing I remember is Father's face as he watched me drag my lame leg after me. Even now, when I catch him looking at me, I know what he sees—a worthless scrap, a waste piece like the blemished poplar he uses where no one will notice, on the bottoms of drawers, the undersides of tables, the tops of chests he will paint over.

While Mother was ill, Father tried to please her by praising my work or—and this always made her smile like a girl at Christmas—saying he thought my bad leg was beginning to straighten and flesh out. But my leg was getting no better than she was. And after she died, one day past Michaelmas last year, he no longer took the trouble to hide his impatience with me. And I no longer had her tender kiss on my head when she bade me good night. Or the sound of her laughter if I added a silly new verse to the songs we used to sing.

Our earliest "concerts" featured a single song, *"Backe, backe, Kuchen,"* "Bake, Bake a Cake." She used to sing that one to me when I was little, as she shaped our griddlecakes by the hearth. *"To bake a cake you need five things, I'm told."* Her voice was light as the bells of the river church, coming to me from above as I sat in the shadow of her skirts. *"Eggs, butter, salt, milk, and cornmeal to make it gold."* Grinning up at her, I sang a different cake for us, one made with worms, toads, mud, and pee to make it gold! When I added my extra ingredients, Mother always reared back her head and laughed. Then she would bend down and scoop me into her arms. "Let us keep that recipe our secret, young man,"

she would say, pinching both my legs till the one I could feel tingled. "I think your father would rather I use cornmeal, after all."

There were more songs, more secrets over the years, and the laughter always bubbling between us. In the end, though, Mother was too weak even to sing. So I did both our parts, singing first the traditional version of an old favorite, like the one where the queen goes riding "all in green, green, green." Next I would sing my version, which featured all the people in our town—the mayor's wife in boots, boots, boots; Papa in sawdust, dust, dust; and Mother in fur, fur, fur. "And where will I get fur?" she asked me once, smiling gamely from her pillows.

I grinned and whispered in her ear. "You know our good neighbor's little dog, the one that keeps yapping all night long?"

Mother put her hand over her mouth, then laughed until she coughed. And coughed until I ran for water. After, she lay breathing so hard I was afraid for her. I hid my fear, but vowed never to make her laugh again.

I cannot explain how such sad memories made my fingers fairly dance over the wood. Perhaps it was because I knew I could not spend the time on this crutch I had lavished on my others. They had each been fashioned in stolen hours, minutes snatched when Father was at church or delivering furniture or running errands. Always, I had the old crutch to make do with until my new one was ready. Now, though, unless I wanted to be carried everywhere, I needed to finish today.

When the armrest was done, I found a pad of fleece to cush-
ion it. I had just put it aside to work on a chest, when Father
burst through the door. He was smiling, noisy and flushed with
triumph. I tried to hide the disappointment that swamped me
when the place was filled with his smell, his great arms sweep-
ing across the room.

"You should have seen the crowd," he said, glancing only
briefly at the chest before me. I had put just one coat of varnish
on it, and the brass fittings still lay scattered on the table. I was
certain he would rage about how little I had accomplished, but
instead he gossiped on.

"It seems I am not the only one who wants to beat some
brains into that muttonhead of a mayor! The council chambers
were full to bursting. The whole town is fed up with the rats."

"Did you tell them about the footstool?" I asked.

"Yes, but that was nothing next to some of the others' stories."
He hung up his cap and jacket, then sat across from me, reaching
by habit for something to work on. As he grabbed a chest, I
pulled my bad leg away from his glance, hiding it under the bench.

"The miller says the vermin have left him nothing to grind.
And one fräulein told how her baby's fingers will not stop bleeding since those infernal pests bit its hand while it slept."

I said nothing, but put the top of my unfinished crutch under the bench as well. I had not shaped the shaft yet, so I would
have to swing myself from bench to table to bed for the rest of
the day. Father was sure to find new work for us after the little
boxes were done.

"I thought we would have to wait all day," Father went on, "while everyone told his tale. I guess the mayor did, too, because suddenly he jabbed one chubby finger into the air and called for silence. 'Good folk,' he said, 'I have heard enough.' He leaned over and whispered to a member of the council, then raised that silly finger again. 'I will hire the piper tomorrow.'

"There surely never was such clapping and shouting. You'd think the old fool was bringing Our Savior to town. He promised to send for the rat-catcher by first light—he even offered to fetch the man himself. You should have heard the stomping and whistling at that, boy."

My father seldom used my name, and I would go days without hearing anyone call me Emmett. The blacksmith's apprentice sometimes shouted, "Hi, there, Emmett!" as I passed the smith's stall, and of course, the children outside the baker's all knew me and my soft heart. "Emmett! Emmett!" they would shriek each time I came for the seeded rolls Father favored. "Give us a crumb, Emmett! Give us a taste!"

"That will be a sight to see," Father was saying now. He had begun work on the chest, his hands moving so expertly with the fittings, he hardly needed to look at all. "I expect the whole town will be in the streets to watch the piper." He raised his eyes to me, and if I saw no fondness there, his expression was at least kind. "We shall take the morning off, boy. I would not want to miss those inky devils skittering out of Hameln."

"I am afraid I would only slow you down, Pater," I said, ashamed. "Unless you will allow me to carve a new crutch

tonight?" I hated the reedy way my voice rose at the end of the question, the way my eyes avoided his.

He barely hesitated. "No need," he told me, waving my concern away with his thick, corded arm. "We will ride in the lumber wagon and have a fine view from there." Nothing, it seemed, would dampen his spirits, not even a crippled son.

Good as his coerced word, our mayor saw to it that the famous rat-catcher came to town the next day. It looked as though a puppet show or a magical healer were expected, so lined with people were the streets around the main square. Father and I, perched atop our wagon, had a clear view over the heads of the crowd: we could see the grand spire of St. Nicolai rising across from us and the pie sellers and candy vendors weaving through the throng. The children who normally haunted the baker's were now stationed behind the pastry seller, dogging his every step like pigeons waiting for him to drop some of the sweet stuff.

I was wishing I had been able to whittle a new crutch, to sneak away and buy a few squares of honey bread for those hungry youngsters, when silence fell on the square. The vendors stopped hawking, the children stopped playing, and everyone turned to look down the road from town hall. There, marching to the strangest, shrillest tune I had ever heard, a man wound his way in and out of side streets, gradually advancing toward the crowd in the square.

His flowing cape winked from red to green to blue as he

moved. His leggings were a bright wheat color, and he wore a small striped cap on his head. By the time he had worked his way to the market square, I could see that his shoulders were broad and his face smiling. I could also see that he was not alone. Behind him, trailing like a long black ribbon in the dirt, were the rats of Hameln. The piper moved briskly across the square but appeared not in the least alarmed, as if there were nothing strange about being followed by an endless parade of rats.

And endless it was. Every rat from every rat hole in the city seemed to have fallen in love with the piper's music. Mice, too, had joined the swarm of small dark bodies that hurried in a steady, squeaking stream after the rat-catcher. As if his whistle pipe had taken ill and could play only in fits and starts, the piper's tune resembled nothing so much as a bout of hiccups, or the whine of wind trapped behind a thick oak door. It faded and swelled, darted and turned, but to the vermin it may as well have been church bells calling them to penance. Like the sinners they were, they rushed by the hundreds—nay, by the thousands— along Market Street past our astonished eyes.

By the time the last rat finally scrambled down the street, the piper had long since disappeared from view. But our holiday did not end there. People began to break from the crowd and rush af- ter the rats to see where the piper would lead them. Father, not to be outdone, flicked the reins across old Patience's back and turned the cart to fall in line with the others. We rode past most of the good citizens of Hameln till we came to the edge of town

and the river. And though we stopped at the shoreline, the piper
and his devil's brigade did not.

Still smiling in between breaths on his pipe, the rat-catcher was
knee-deep in the chilly water of the Weser. He continued to play
the strange music and the rats continued to follow him—right into
the water. They leapt with a will into the river, paddled briefly,
then sank with a chorus of sharp, outraged shrieks. Soon the
water was black with them, chopped to a froth with their desperate splashing. The air around us rang with the shouts of
everyone on shore. Father threw his cap against the sky, and I
yelled until I was hoarse. It felt grand, indeed, to see the end of
those long-tailed nightmares and to have something to cheer
about at last.

It was not two days later that Father went back to see the mayor.
The tax collector had paid us a visit and been turned away. "The
rats are gone," Father told the man, who despite his huge girth
seemed reluctant to demand what he'd come for. "Why should I
give you money now?"

"The mayor promised the rat-catcher," the collector said.
"Only yesterday, he gave his word."

"Then he should have given his money, too." Father shut the
door in the poor man's face, rubbed his hands on his apron, and
returned to work. But when the blacksmith and the baker decided to complain to the mayor that he was asking for too much

money, Father took off his apron again and went with them. I was not sorry to see him go. The trip to town hall would surely give me time to finish my crutch. Hobbling as I was from place to place, I missed my wooden leg!

As it happened, I could have fashioned two crutches while Father was away. I worked happily for several hours, even adding a chain of grazing sheep along the shaft. Then, instead of wondering what was keeping him, I set off for the baker's the minute I was finished. As always, the beggar children were waiting in the alley by the shop. When I came out with a loaf for Father and me and a bag of buns for them, they sent up a great hurrah and gathered around me, all talking at once. "Here, Emmett!" one boy in a dirty vest cried. "Look how skinny I am!" He opened the vest and lifted his shirt to show me his belly. "Emmett, that's nothing," a smaller boy yelled. "That pig's belly is a mountain compared to my hungry stomach." He closed his eyes and sucked in the flesh under his ribs.

The girls in the group rolled their eyes but could not keep from laughing. They weren't about to show their bellies, so they tried a different tack: "How rude these ruffians are!" a girl named Gretchen scolded. Taller than most of the boys, she was not above cuffing the younger ones when they misbehaved. "If you want a sweet, your talk must be sweet," she told them, then turned to me. "Oh, Herr Emmett," she whined in a high, thin voice nothing like her normal tone. "How kind of you to buy those buns." She bent her long frame into a deep, awkward curtsy. "May I try one, pretty please?"

But it was Ilse, as usual, who won the first piece. She stood quietly in the middle of the pack, a shy little thing in a black cape and bonnet. When I dangled a raisin-filled bun above the rowdy crew, she did not raise her hands like the rest, though her hungry eyes followed the treat. So of course, I tore off a good half of the little cake and gave it to her. "Here, fräulein," I said, bowing from my crutch. *"Gott segne Dich."* God bless you.

Some of these children, I knew, had parents who sent them out to beg while they themselves spent the day drinking in the Green Boar or picking the pockets of those who did. Others had been orphaned or abandoned when their parents died or were sent to jail. These unfortunates tagged along with the rest for protection. But Ilse had a mother, she always made sure to tell me, who neither drank nor robbed. *"Mein mutter sie wird zu himmel gehen."* My mother is going to heaven. The poor woman, it seemed, was too ill to leave her bed, and like my own mother at the last, lay patiently waiting for the coughing to stop and her pain to end.

Ilse took the cake now and, as I might have expected, tore a generous portion off to give to a squalling infant in another girl's arms. They were like a family, these orphans and runaways, a tiny family that looked after its own. I knew it was a sin, but sometimes I envied the beggar children. I had a warm bed and a father who taught me a trade, but I had no littermates, no warm bodies to jostle and nest against.

Father came back home well satisfied, whistling as he hung his coat and cap by the door, took up his apron, and tied it around his waist.

Though I would never have dared whistle out loud, I was whistling, too—inside, where my little beggars had lifted my spirits. The children had all admired my new crutch. Not only was it sturdy and just the right size, but the carving was surely my finest: the sweep of wings, the cut-out mountains on the armrest, and then, along the shaft, a shepherd leading his flock down from the foothills. I could not help but feel pride when the ragamuffins gathered round, touching it as if it were a relic in church. How Ilse had laughed as she counted the sheep and followed their tracks with her tiny finger!

I used the crutch now to make my way to our hearth, though I ran the risk of Father's making a joke of the "curlicues and doo-dads" with which I'd decorated it. "And what did he say, the mayor?" I asked, hooking a small pot above the flames. It was well past suppertime, and the church bells had rung twice since I'd lit the candles.

"The old fool," Father told me, bent over the last of the four chests. "He sings whichever way the wind blows."

I could not cook griddlecakes the way Mother used to, but cornmeal mush made a fine supper with roasted turnips. Not that Father would taste the food, anyway. He always ate like a human whirlwind, sucking up whatever was on his plate, belching after and stumbling to bed.

"Once I persuaded him that the rat-catcher could not very well summon dead rats back from the river," Father said, looking extremely pleased with himself, "he agreed there was no need to pay so much as he had promised.

"In fact," he added, turning the chest, applying varnish with his smallest brush, "I warrant he has decided not to pay him at all."

"But the rat-catcher worked the whole morning," I said. Father surely knew what it was like to have hours of labor go for nothing. Wasn't that why he had gone to the mayor in the first place?

He shook his shaggy head now, shoved the finished chest toward me. "Did you see me smile even once, boy, when I was fitting the lock on this box?" He stood up to take off his apron, then came to the table where I'd set out our bowls. "Do you see me asking good folk to pay me for a pipe dance?"

"But the rats, even the mice, they . . ."

"Those vermin were chased here by that rat-catcher," Father said. "It was all part of his plan to fleece the town."

"Still," I told him, "they are gone now. The piper kept his part of the bargain."

"He kept it with magic. Those rats were under a spell." Father brought his bowl to the fire, held it out for me to fill. "For all we know, that spell caster is in league with the devil. Would you have me help Satan earn his keep, boy?"

There was nothing to say. It mattered little whether the piper

was a heavenly messenger or the devil's own son. Father would not be persuaded to pay for help he no longer needed. We finished our meal in silence and went to our beds the same way.

It was three days later, on St. Paul and St. John's feast day, when the piper came back to Hameln. The mayor gave him no money, and the rest of the council scolded him for trying to do business on a feast day. Then they all hurried off to church. Which is where Father and I were when the rat-catcher followed his debtors into the great nave of St. Nicolai. The mass was beginning, and we two had just found a bench in back when the piper strode in the door. He made his way down an aisle in the direction of the altar. I watched him stop at the seventh station of the cross, glance briefly at the council members who had taken seats up front, and then look up at the statue of Our Fallen Savior.

The piper, in that moment, bore little resemblance to the smiling magician who had played the rats down our streets only days before. Older, wearier, he looked as pained and tormented as the image above him on the Way of Sorrow. By the time he woke from his sad trance, the councilmen had all closed their eyes and assumed pious expressions. The piper turned on his heel and went back to the street.

Underneath the chants for mass, I heard a different music start up in the square outside. Though it sounded faint as fairy tunes, something in this lively melody made me restless. After a

while I could bear it no longer and, bracing my crutch against the bench, rose from my seat. Father was used to my standing so as not to pain my bad leg. When I left his side and walked out the door, he remained unmoving and still, so still I suspected he had fallen asleep.

If the music had been faint in the church, it was not much louder in the open air. It sounded like a melody played a great distance away, and so it proved to be. A crowd of children—from toddlers carried by their brothers and sisters to boys and girls of twelve summers—hurried past me on the road out of town toward the mountains. I looked ahead of them and saw a line of children, wide as the road, stretching from the gates of the city into the hills.

I shook my head, wondering what could be drawing them away, when my little family of beggars rushed by. "Come on, Emmett!" they cried. "You will miss it all if you do not run." They buzzed past me like a swarm of bees headed for the hive. Only Ilse and a tall boy named Heinrich stayed behind.

"You will never keep up with your bad leg, Emmett, sir," Ilse said, studying me with sad, grown-up eyes.

"He is too old to go, anyway," Heinrich told her. "Come on, Ilse, or we, too, will be left behind."

"Wait!" I hobbled after them. "What is it? What is that music?"

Ilse hung on my crutch, jumping with eagerness. "You see? He hears it." She pulled and tugged me ahead. "Emmett can come, too."

"But the piper said . . ." Henrich turned, talking as he walked backwards toward the peaks of the Weserbergland.

"How old are you, Emmett, sir?" Ilse unfastened herself from my crutch, tried pushing me from behind.

"Nearly fifteen," I told her, suddenly feeling that my age was something to be ashamed of.

"I told you." Heinrich turned back to face the mountains. "He is too old. The piper said only children could hear his song."

"I cannot hear it well," I told them, stopping to listen again. The piper's music swelled from far away, but it sounded sweet today, not at all like the brisk high-pitched tune with which he had lured the rats.

"Emmett is our friend," Ilse announced. "He must come with us. He will share the food and new clothes."

"Food?" I asked. "Clothes?"

"Yes," Ilse told me. "Can you not hear it in the music?" She cocked her pretty head to one side, as if she held a seashell to her ear. "There will be more than we can ever eat if we go with him, Emmett." She smiled, her whole body alert, eager. "And firewood for Mama. And a medicine to cure her cough."

"And puppets," added Heinrich. "I hear a puppet show. There will be benches to watch it on, and no one will kick us away because we lack coins."

"I hear milk for all the babies," Ilse said. "And new shoes with no holes!"

"There is all this in that music?" I hobbled faster, my face to

the mountains. But I despaired of keeping up with the rest. Then, as we passed our street, I remembered the lumber cart. "Wait here, Ilse," I said. "We shall catch the piper yet."

By the time I had harnessed old Patience and ridden the cart to the spot I'd left them, Heinrich had gone on ahead and only Ilse remained. I pulled her up next to me and we took off at a good pace. As we traveled through the huge gates that guard our town, we passed others along the road, and they begged rides, too. Soon the cart was packed with little ones, laughing and waving their hands at those who must walk. We moved more slowly now, but at last I heard the music grow louder.

When we caught up to the piper, he had marched the children through the open fields and into the foothills of the mountains. He put down his pipe to survey the line of young ones still snaking its way out of town. I, too, turned to see them, and the sight took my breath away. I had not realized how many children lived in Hameln, but here they all were! It looked like an army, like the children's crusade that had gone to fight the infidels when my grandfather was a boy. Granddad had loved to tell how the children across Germany and France dropped their milk pails and hoes to take up swords and shields.

There were no swords in the ranks that filled the winding road from Hameln, but surely that small army marched with as good a will. On sturdy legs, they came hurrying to join us, and those who were too young to walk were carried by those who were not. I could have varnished a dozen chests in the time it

took them to move to our position in the foothills. When they had, a great hush fell over them all as the piper raised his hand to speak.

I pulled the cart as close as I could, and by picking up a few of the children who had crept nearer still, we were able at last to be no more than a few yards from the man who had saved Hameln from the rats. He was not dressed in the gay costume he had worn before; instead, he was clad in green, like a hunter. He sported no cap, but wore a cape with a great clasp that gleamed in the sun. *"Kinder,"* he said. Children. "Your parents are in church. They seem to believe they need not live a holy life so long as they bend their knees at mass." His smile, like a mischievous child's, belied his harsh words. "But I bear you no ill will on their behalf. In fact, I hope to spare you the hardships that have fixed themselves like barnacles to the souls of your elders."

He finished speaking, then took up his pipe and played a short tune. His music was no longer faint, but as clear as if I had leaned over a tumbling falls and was letting the roar fill my ears. I wasn't sure what the piper's words meant, but his music made a picture in my head. I saw deep woods broken by a single ray of sun piercing it from overhead. A bird, like the ones on my crutch, flew out of a tree and called to me.

Then the music stopped and the piper spoke again. "Love and song are your birthrights," he told us. "Like good Moses, I have come to lead you out from this hard Egypt to a place where you shall have both." He lifted his pipe once more to his lips and, though I cannot say how, played a chain of notes that sounded

like laughter. For a dizzy moment, time melted away and I was holding my mother's skirts, smiling into her surprise. *Toads in our cake, Emmett? What will Papa say?*

As I listened, the music turned slower, sadder. Now—perhaps it was in the way the piper rolled his fingertips across the stops—the notes sounded like sighs. Their softness made me think of Mother again, but this time I remembered her voice, how it was thin as a whisper in those last, lost days: *And where will I get fur?*

"In the place I am taking you, lambkins," the Piper told us, putting aside his pipe for the third time, "it is always spring, and buds are forever new. Nothing grows old and sour. No one is cold or hungry or lame." At this last, a few young ones turned to look at me, but I did not mind being singled out. It felt almost like an honor, as if my bad leg had earned me this moment.

When the rat-catcher ended his speech and headed up the steep wall of rock ahead of us, his tune changed again. It trickled from his pipe like a sweet May drink that made us want more with every sip.

I do not know what the others on the path below us heard in that song, but I know each child in our cart found something different in the ditty. One boy laughed like a yipping pup, shouting that it announced a holiday for apprentices; another said the tune would take us to the other side of the mountains, where a great ship with a crew of child sailors lay in port; poor Gretchen insisted the piper was playing a palace, where she would wear gowns with jeweled bodices and diadems in her hair. I looked at

the beggar girl's tangled mop and almost laughed out loud, but Ilse cupped my chin in both her hands and turned my face to hers.

Flushed and eager, the little girl was more alive than I had ever seen her. "Come, Emmett!" she cried. "The piper is playing Mama's cure. If we follow, I will see her healthy and warm."

It was clear we could not ride up the cliffs. Old Patience was already silver with sweat, and even a billy goat could not have dragged Father's cart across that rocky slope. "We shall have to go on foot from here," I told the children. Forgetting that I was not a goat but only a one-legged boy, I hoisted myself to the ground and held up my arms for Ilse. She found my crutch and lay it in my hands instead. That was when it first occurred to me that I might not be able to follow the others.

I was swamped with a familiar loneliness, the ancient hurt of someone who has always watched while others ran and played, just out of reach. As the rat-catcher scrambled nimbly up the rock, playing all the while, I saw where he was leading everyone. Not with my eyes, since nothing was visible beyond the crest of the mountain. But the place came clear to me, as sharp and real as wind on a hilltop.

In the land the piper played, everyone flew. On wings wide as banners, radiant and fine as sunlight, young and old traveled effortlessly through the air. My mother was in his song, but she was no longer pale and coughing. Instead, she soared between clouds and birds, waving as she looked down at me and the mountains below. I waved back, already straining upward, feel-

ing my own wings sprouting from my back. Even as I dug my crutch into the rocks strewn along my way, new wings, like two sweetly burning kisses, worked their way through my shoulder blades. Mama smiled encouragement and opened her arms, while those tender, feathered buds began to uncurl and lift me above the earth.

But not soon enough. For while the other children following the piper used both hands to haul themselves over boulders and swing across ravines toward the piper's music, I kept hold of my crutch. Though the rat-catcher's tune gave me wings, they were only a promise, a dream of what I would be when the piper led us home. I did not, could not, throw away my third leg just yet. Soon all the children except Ilse had left me behind.

"Do not worry, Herr Emmett," the faithful girl told me. She worked her little body under my free arm like a second crutch and tried to lift me over the narrow, winding gorge carved by a now vanished stream. "I will help you." She followed the piper's progress with longing eyes but would not leave me to fend for myself. With each small advance we made, I could see the end of the line of children moving further into the distance and hear my little friend's sighs grow longer and more forlorn.

Finally I could bear it no more. "Ilse," I told her, "you must leave me and go on." I had the pledge of the music to keep me company, and the vision of my wings. I brandished my crutch like a sword. "I will meet you up ahead."

"*Nein*, Herr Emmett." The yearning for her own dream was still in her eyes and voice, but she would not forsake me. She

only adjusted my weight across her tiny shoulder and set out again for the ledge where the piper had come to a stop. "We are almost there."

Four more times, before we reached the others, I begged Ilse to go ahead. And four more times she refused. The piper was stationed above us, playing a sweet, jolly tune that gave us both fresh hope. But when we had at last caught up to the others, even his music could not keep my good leg from trembling like the bad. I was unable to take another step. "Here we are at last," I panted, throwing myself on a small grassy space between boulders. "Hurry up! I will come as soon as I have got my breath again."

Ilse raised her eyes to the mossy crag above the crowd of young ones. There stood the piper, guarding the entrance to a mountain cave. Many of Hameln's children, even my little beggars, had told me how they played in such caves, how they followed dark tunnels to underground rivers or to the sudden light and flowers of mountain meadows. Which is why, when the ratcatcher smiled and walked into the cave, not one of the children was afraid to follow.

He remained just inside the entrance, now waving the children in, now playing his sprightly marching tune. Soon nearly the whole crowd had walked into the cave—big brothers carried little ones, friends raced arm in arm, stragglers picked up their pace and dashed toward the black hole in the mountain. Each of them raced for the dream the song had promised them, each sure they were only steps from making it come true. On they

marched, looking for grand meals and new shoes, dead parents and lost sisters, ball games that would never end and dolls that could grow up with their owners. Beds of lace and silver dishes, talking dogs and smiling moons and rivers full of fish that caught and cooked themselves.

The piper stayed just inside the cave's mouth, waving to each child who passed. All the while he kept playing and all the while wings fluttered in my head and heart. "Go on, now," I told Ilse. I struggled to my feet and settled onto my crutch again, even though I could feel a blister where it rubbed under my arm. "I will follow fast behind."

Making sure she could keep me in sight, the little girl scam-pered off. At first she stopped every few steps, to turn and wave, waiting until I had waved back before going on. Finally, though, the music set her running and she did not stop until she reached the cave. I watched her bow shyly to the rat-catcher, watched him pause his tune for the briefest moment as he bent his head to whisper something in her ear. Whatever it was, it made her smile—no demure lass's smile, but a broad grin fit for any care-less boy. That smile was the last I saw of Ilse. She turned to bid me make haste, then raced eagerly after the rest.

I was nearly alone outside the cave. Besides me, only a girl my own age and a toddler had not yet scaled the hill to the piper. And if the piper's music had not shown me my heart's desire, had not sounded like wings and my mother's laughter, I would have let those two stragglers climb the last rise without me. My arm had been rubbed raw by the new crutch and the arduous climb.

At last, though I had to follow a good distance behind the girls, all three of us stood before the rat-catcher. Up close, he was even more handsome than he had seemed from afar. His countenance was lined and dark from the sun, but his features were noble. He looked at me with such warmth that I was astonished when he put down his pipe and barred us from the cave's entrance. "I am sorry, indeed," he told us, "that you have come all this way. But you may go no further."

At first I could not believe his words and persisted in trying to enter the cave as the others had before us. It was not until he braced his hand on my chest that I stopped trying to slip by him.

"You are grown past twelve," the piper said, not unkindly. "It is too late for you." He stared at me, taking my measure as if he planned to fit me with stockings and a cape. "Perhaps it is for the best, after all. The way is long on the other side. You have the heart for it, but not the legs."

"As for you two," he told the girls who stood fast by the cave, clutching each other's hands, "the wonders that wait yonder are only for the little one." He turned to the older girl. "Go home with this lad. Your parents will be glad of your return."

I wanted to tell him about the wings I had felt sprouting from my back, about the place where legs would not be needed. But he was already pushing the two of us from the cave, and though his dusky face had turned sad, his voice was firm: "Be a good fellow now and lead this lass back home."

The smaller girl tried to reach her sister from behind the

piper, while the older one wept, begging him to let her go with the rest. It was not until she and I had been forced back onto the path outside the cave that I realized her eyes were of no use to her. Instead of scrambling up the path, she remained pressed against the rocky sides of the cave, trying to feel her way back the way we'd come.

"I want to see," the girl wailed as she walked. "Please, let me see."

But the piper turned his back on us, withdrew into the cave, and raised his hands. As if he had pulled down the cover of a stall or drawn the curtain on a puppet stage, the stone wall of the cave began to thicken and cover the entrance. Bit by bit, the hole sealed itself up, and though I raced back and beat my crutch against the rock, there was no stopping it. Soon there was nothing left but the moss-covered face of the mountain. It was as if it had stood that way for hundreds of years, as if there had never been a cave there at all.

The line of children that returned to Hameln that afternoon was a good deal shorter than the one which had set out in the morning. The blind girl, whose name was Berta, and I moved slowly, inching our way back to town. This time, of course, there was no music to urge us on, and my good leg had begun to throb, so that the poor girl's leaning on me made each step more painful than the last.

Berta told me she had stolen away from home without telling

her mother. She had persuaded her little sister to come with her, but now feared what her parents might do when she returned. "I heard the music," she said, "and felt I would die if I did not follow the others. But now I have lost my little darling and must live all alone in the dark."

She stopped to wipe her tears, then leaned on me once more. My leg nearly folded under the renewed weight, but in truth I had begun to feel less sorry for myself. I could see, after all, and could walk where I pleased, slow as I was.

"I am happy for my sister, but what is to become of me, Emmett?" Berta seemed to grow more frantic as we drew toward the city gates. "My mother keeps me like a linnet in a cage. I am never allowed outside the house unless my sister takes my hand."

Sure enough, once I had guided her back to the small house from which she had snuck away at dawn, a woman rushed out and, without a word to me, hurried Berta inside. I never saw her again.

As for *my* homecoming, Father was clearly relieved when I walked through the door. "Good!" he said. "I have a new order for three stools and a hope chest." He set the work out between us on the bench. "I told the smith that thieving rat-catcher wouldn't want a cripple."

I did not bother to ask who might best be called a thief, the piper or the men who had refused to pay him. Instead, I kept my silence. For once, I looked forward to working at the bench, to a long stretch of hours during which I would not have to put my good leg to the test or lean my sore arm across my crutch.

As we set about the new orders, Father told me how the entire town was in an uproar, how all the mothers and fathers had missed their children after church. How they had scoured the streets until a nursemaid and two mothers reported that all the little ones had run after the piper. The women had called and called, had chased after the children, but the youngsters had hidden from them, then scampered out of sight.

When I confessed that I, too, had followed the piper, Father paid me more mind than he ever had before. He held my eyes while I talked, took in every word. He asked question after question, then decided he must visit the mayor once more. "We will send men into the cave," he said. "We will catch that wizard and make him sorry he ever set foot in Hameln."

But you know how it turned out, don't you? Everyone for leagues around has heard the story. The cave has not been found, nor has a single child returned to Hameln. All the parents are in mourning and the street down which the piper led his children's army has been renamed. Now we call it *"Bunelose Gasse,"* the street of silence. The council has passed a law that no singing or music be allowed there, not that anyone feels like singing or playing music, anyway. Hameln is a ghost town, with no little ones chasing down the roads, pleading for pennies to spend at the market or laughing and clapping at the puppet shows. My small beggar friends no longer wait for me by the baker's, no longer suck

in their stomachs to prove how much room they have for cakes and buns.

There are other boys and girls my own age left here, but none younger than twelve. So we are half what we were, forlorn and sorrowful, though some of the parents have not given up hope. Even now, a full year since the piper led the children away, they light candles and place them in the front windows of their houses each night. Sometimes, when I am coming back from errands, I look up to see lonely shadows standing watch at all these windows. Our churches are filled to overflowing with mothers and fathers praying that their sons and daughters will be restored to them. Two crosses of white stone have been erected in the foothills outside the city gates, one on each side of the place where Berta's little sister and I saw the entrance to the cave.

As for Berta, her mother guards her so closely now, she is not even allowed in church. When Father sends me out with the wagon, I always drive past her house in hopes of talking to her. But all I see is a shadow peering from behind the windows, a shadow I fancy is Berta, waiting for another chance to run away.

And me? My good leg has not recovered from my climb up the mountain. It pains me often now, and Father says I am useless. Perhaps he is right, for I am grown sickly, too, like my mother. Sometimes I burn more wood than I work, sitting by the fire and shivering, even when the day is warm.

I have not forgotten the song of wings or the place the piper's music promised me. I remember every note, and I sing them over

to myself when I am feeling well enough to work at the bench. I do not know if such a paradise exists or if, as the town fathers all say, the rat-catcher fooled the children and marched them into slavery. Ilse's dream, you see, never came true. Her mother died a few weeks after Ilse and the others disappeared. I went to see her once. I told her how Ilse longed for her to get well, but she only sighed and turned her face to the wall. Magic and life are both like God's will, impossible to understand.

I have put words to the rat-catcher's melody, words that speak what his pipe played. *"Every hope you've ever hoped, every dream you've dreamed."* It is a song I dare not sing aloud, but it is seldom out of my heart. *"Every plan you've ever planned, every scheme you've schemed."* Now and then, Father looks at me darkly, as if he knows what I am thinking. "Sit up straight," he growls. He shakes his head and nods at my leg, propped on a stool to keep it from throbbing. "You have carved too deep there," he will say, pointing. Or, "Do you want to shame me with that finish?"

I do not care. I draw my leg under the table and bend over my work so he cannot see my face. I keep singing, inside, where only I can hear. When I come to the part about rising off the ground like an egret, about letting my legs dangle in the sky, I feel those two burning kisses again on my back.

He who dares to follow me,
he who dares to fly,
shall set the wind against his breast,
shall see with God's own eye.

I swear to you, my new wings start to sprout, to unfurl in that small, close room where I work under my father's scornful gaze. The certainty comes stealing over me then, a tingling bright and clear as the bells of St. Bonifatius. Once more the piper promises me, once more the pledge is made—it will not be long before I, too, have flown away.

Mother Love

The first thing she noticed was that she wasn't cold anymore. When she opened her eyes to see if someone had stoked the fire, there was a pair of bare feet on the earthen floor in front of her. She had fallen asleep over the mending, and her fingers tingled, either from wearing a thimble too long or from the spectacular warmth that filled the whole room.

Gretel knew it was her angel even before she looked up, even though when she did, there were no wings. Or perhaps, she thought afterward, they had been folded behind, where she couldn't see. The figure standing in their tiny cottage looked at once astonishing and familiar. Though the body was taller, stronger than she remembered, the face was the same, and the eyes—the eyes that studied Gretel with head-to-toe delight. And just as she had each time her angel came to her, Gretel wanted more than anything to reach out, to touch the shining skin, the long transparent robes. But she couldn't bear to frighten the vision away and to find her hands empty, clutching air.

So she sat still, basking in the warmth and a steady, low sound that was like the humming of crickets, though it was long

past the season when those tiny noisemakers rubbed their legs together to announce spring. It was as if everything around her—the small table, the fire in the hearth, even the bedrolls under the window ledge—was buzzing like bees, whispering in the language of birch or flame or sweet hay. *Mother,* the table said. *Mother,* spoke the fire and the hay. *Mother.*

When Hansel slammed through the door and staggered in under a mountain of cordwood, the whispering died and the angel melted away. "Are your ears stopped, girl?" he asked, spilling the logs by the fire, wiping his face with his sleeve. "I told you I would kick the door when I had the wood ready."

Blinking, Gretel willed back the angel, the tiny voices. But there was only Hansel, filling the room with cold air and resentment. "I did not hear you, Brother," she told him. "I was . . . sewing."

"Ay," he said. "Inside, where it is dry and warm. While I was splitting wood with no gloves."

She wanted to make it up to him. She always wanted to make it up. "I saw something, Hansel. Something beautiful." If she could help him see it, if he could share the splendor, maybe he would feel warmer.

"And what was that, Sister?" He looked out the tiny window to make certain their parents weren't nearby, then threw himself, full-length, in front of the hearth. "Still more heavenly nonsense? More messengers with wings?"

She picked up her mending, told the cloth instead of him. "I could not see the wings this time," she said. "But there was such

a feeling of peace in the house, Hansel. I know Mother was nearby, and I know Father will come back with good news."

Hansel rolled onto his stomach but sat up suddenly, his fingers to his lips. "Not a word of your visions, girl." He scrambled to his feet and set about stacking the logs of wood. "Do you hear?"

Gretel nodded, but as the door opened and their father and stepmother tossed empty bags onto the floor, she knew there was no good news. And the feeling she'd had, the glimpse of a mother she had nearly forgotten, faded. Their stepmother, bigger, louder, ten times more real, sighed theatrically, then unwrapped the straps of wool from her ankles and put her shoes by the fire. Their father walked to the hearth, rubbing his hands, his face furrowed with disappointment. "Not even beans," he said. "Not even a stale loaf."

It was the third time this week the pair had taken Gretel's sewing to market, the third time they had been turned away by merchants unwilling to part with food in return for the girl's dainty-work. "We cannot go on like this, you know." The children's stepmother was named Prudence, but she was more stingy than wise. "I have said it over and over. Four are too many mouths to feed." She glared at the children, who stood still and light on their feet, like birds ready to fly. "Especially when these two do nothing to earn their keep."

"I could help Hansel with the chopping, mistress." Gretel looked at her brother, so exhausted he could barely stand, at her own mending and sewing, folded into a careful pile on the table.

"We could sell extra wood that way. Or I might stitch hats in place of aprons?" Despite all their work, her stepmother was bleeding anger, and Gretel needed to stanch the flow. "We will do better tomorrow." It was what her mother had said, day after day, when she was sick. *I will be better tomorrow.*

"Tomorrow," Prudence told her, closing her eyes against the heartbreak of their day, "we may all starve to death." She looked hard at her husband, harder still at Gretel. "And unless you plan on cooking them, girl, your hats will not fill our empty bellies."

The image of their stuffing coarse wool in their mouths hung over the table when they sat down to supper. The meal, which was nothing but water seasoned with the dried mushrooms Gretel had gathered in the fall and small pieces of the moldy bread they had been too proud to eat the night before, did not last long. It was eaten in silence and ended when their father stood suddenly, hurled his spoon into the fire, and did something neither of his children had ever heard him do before: he swore.

"Christ's blood!" His voice cracked, then trembled on the edge of tears. "A rat would not eat this slop!" Without meeting the eyes of anyone at the table, he picked up his jacket, sodden with snow, and walked out the cottage door.

As soon as he was gone, Hansel raced to the hearth. He grabbed the poker and nudged his father's spoon out of the flames. It was only a little twisted and would still serve. No one spoke until Prudence rose and began moving their chairs from the table.

"Best sweep and put the bed things out," she told Gretel. Her

tone was almost gentle in its shock. "I will fetch your father before he freezes."

When the bowls and spoons were rubbed clean and the pallets placed on the floor, their parents came back inside, Father still avoiding their glance, Prudence set and stiff as beaten cream. Hansel stoked the fire, and they all four lay down in silence until Father's snoring started at last. Gretel lay awake, listening to the ragged rhythm it made, waiting for the call of the owl that always set up its night vigil in the poplar outside their door.

The angel who visited her in dreams seemed more intense, more real than the visions she saw during the day. At night, she could feel its breath, like wind across a meadow; sometimes it would touch her, sending a shiver through her whole body, the shock of grace. It was the same way she'd felt when another hand, moist and burning with fever, had stroked her hair. *I have already seen heaven, Gret,* Mother had told her. *It looks just like you.*

While the rest of the family stumbled from their pallets, grumbling, fighting their way into morning, Gretel always woke smiling. The dreams were like a small bird, a tiny heartbeat she kept warm against her chest.

So when her parents' voices woke her that night, she came unwillingly from the lip of a dream, a scene in which her angel threw sparkling stones along their path, leaving twisting trails of gems behind them. She sat in the dark, brushing hair from her eyes and listening to the angry talk.

"You must do it tomorrow," she heard her stepmother say. "Take them deep into the forest and leave them there."

And Father answered, weary, frightened. "I cannot, Pru. I will ne'er do such a thing. What would become of them?"

"What will become of *us*, man?" Prudence's voice forgot caution, spiraled toward hysteria. "Would you choose your children over your wife?" Then in the space left by her unanswered question, "Your wife, who can bear you other babes." Lower now, almost a purr, "*Our* own children, not hers."

"Lord Jesus, help me," Father said. "Would you nail me to the cross of an old love? Hansel and the girl are mine, Pru. I will not leave them to starve."

"Then give them the rest of the bread. Give them whatever you will. Only take them deep enough they'll not find their way back."

"How will they fend?"

"Like any two hungry beasts, Husband. Better than four."

Torn from her dream, Gretel felt cold and wretched. *An old love,* her father said. Had he forgotten how he wept by their mother's bed? Had he no memory of the times before, the way he and Mama danced for them, how she whirled, pink-cheeked, then fell against him? *Enough! If you spin me more, you may shake my good sense out. The babes will have no ma, I shall run off with the gypsies and howl at the moon!* Their mother had always looked at Hansel and Gretel then, winking. And when Gretel obligingly gasped and ran to block the door, Mama would go to her and hold her tight. *Well, then,* she'd say each time, *I suppose the gypsies would not mind if you came along, too.*

Now Gretel crawled across the shadows to Hansel's pallet. She shoved his shoulder and when he startled put her hand over his mouth to make him listen. They both heard it then. The plan to pretend a trip for better firewood, a trip that would end with the children abandoned miles from home, left to the mercy of God and wild wolves.

Neither slept, and sunrise found them pale and drawn. While Prudence hummed over a small knapsack and their father sharpened the axes, Hansel fumed. "How dare they?" he whispered to his sister. "Does all the wood I've chopped count for nothing?" His face was as flushed as if he had already been outside in the frosty morning. "Or the rabbits I caught last spring?"

"Do not fret, Brother," Gretel told him. "Our angel will save us." And before he could laugh, before he could daunt her with that scornful look of his, she told him about the dream. "Can you not see? If we drop stones as we go and wait until the moon comes up, our way home will be lit by heaven itself!"

He did not laugh. Instead, he lowered his chin nearly to his chest and squinted with the effort to imagine what she had described. When he raised his head to look at her, his eyes were narrow, calculating. "Mayhap," was all he said.

What neither of them had counted on, of course, was the storm their homecoming caused. That night, they waited until the moon was high enough to light the stones Gretel had sewn like seeds as their parents led them deeper and deeper into the forest.

And when they arrived at the cottage well after dark, there was only one person glad to see them again. "Praise the Savior!" Their father hugged each of them in turn, grinning like a fool. "Look how Providence has seen fit to spare you!"

But Prudence saw less to celebrate. Much less. "What trick did you use?" She turned on Gretel and her brother as if walking home was devil's work, as if they had no right to share the roof under which they'd been born and raised. "Tomorrow we will go further. Tomorrow you will stay where you are put."

So there was no pretense now, no talk of gathering firewood, of the two adults leaving to gather it up while the children napped by the fire. Despite Father's pleas and the children's arguments, their stepmother was determined. "Whether you go or we," she said, "matters little. We will all be better off, with fewer hungry mouths to fill.

"But since your good father and I have kept you fed and dressed till now, it is only right that you be the ones to repay this debt by trying your fortunes in the world."

"Their *fortunes!*" Father sounded hoarse and sharp, a baited bear with no way out. "What fortunes can they find in a land wasted by drought and famine?"

"What if we won't go?" Hansel folded his arms and braced himself as he did when he chopped wood. "What if we refuse to be pushed into the cold?"

"Refuse all you wish," Prudence told him. "Stay here and watch your father starve." She rushed out of Father's grasp and

turned on the boy. "You are certain to outlast him, you know. He is old and tired from working to keep you in firewood and soup." A flame fanned itself to life in her narrow eyes. "And mark me, when he weakens and dies, the two of you will earn a place in hell."

"Pru, you must not say such a thing," Father told her.

But Prudence ignored him and shifted her attention to Gretel. "Ay, you shall find yourselves near enough to the devil's throne to kiss his horny feet." Reluctantly, she unfolded the two bedrolls she had stashed by the hearth. As the girl bent to help her, she studied Gretel's small shoulders, down-turned head. "Make no mistake, ungrateful wretch. You will murder the good man as surely as if you took that ax"—she pointed to the long-handled ax in the hearth corner—"to his throat and did the job clean."

And so the four of them set out for the woods again next morning, the children lagging spiritlessly behind their parents. Neither of them scattered stones, for they both felt the stinging truth of their stepmother's words. If the family stayed together, they were all likely to perish. But if Hansel and Gretel took their chances in the wide world, their youth and daring might somehow earn their keep.

"If he finds a bone," Hansel told his sister as they trudged through the thickening forest, "she will suck it dry, then give

him the leavings." He nodded toward Prudence, and Gretel wondered if he remembered the last day, the day Mama called the two
of them to her. *Take care of your da,* she had said, kissing them
both. *Love him as I have loved you.* She'd curled on her side then,
as if she were taking a nap. Gretel could still see the sharp curve
of her back, the way her poor bones showed through her shift.

So at first when Prudence came into their lives, cleaning and
scrubbing and scolding only a little, it seemed as though Mama
might have sent her. Father's spirits lifted, and he even began to
sing again. Sometimes Prudence laughed and joined in, though
she never danced with Da the way their mother had.

"It may not be long before she turns him out as well." Hansel
threw a stick he had picked up into a small stream. It landed with
a dull thud against the ice. "We will have company on our death
march, eh?"

Apparently, though, their father had other plans. When they
had traveled deeper into the forest than any of them had ever been
and the children lay beside a meager fire, he gathered up his axes
and the knapsack he shared with Prudence. But before he left, he
leaned to whisper in Gretel's ear. "You shall find your way home
again tonight," he told her, pretending only to kiss her farewell.
Then, bending to the boy's ear, too, he added quickly, "The bread
crumbs, lad. Follow the crumbs as you did the stones."

When the older pair had finally disappeared into the woods,
the younger sat up and told each other what they'd heard. Gretel
jumped to her feet, raced to the edge of the pale light cast by the

fire, and then shouted to her brother. "Father spoke true, Hansel," she cried. "Come look at what he has left for us."

She would tell it years from now, over and over. How the trail of crumbs Father had dropped from his loaf led away from the fire. Led the two children, laughing and hopeful once more, back along a winding trail between the oaks and linden, the alder and the elms. Led them for a joyous, buoyant hour, before it dwindled and then disappeared, before the children realized that birds and squirrels had found the bread sooner than they. She hadn't wanted to discourage Hansel, but the spot where the crumbs stopped was such a dark and desolate one, and she had been so looking forward to the warmth of their hearth, that Gretel sat upon the damp ground and cried.

For once her brother did not mock her but sat down beside her, silent, tearless. It seemed less out of tenderness than fatigue and a certain weary patience with her moods. But when she had cried out all her hurt and disappointment, he stood and held out his hand. "Come on, then," he told her. "We are no worse off than we expected to be when we set out this morning."

It was true enough. And as they walked slowly, taking their cues from the angle at which the setting sun poked through the thicket of branches overhead, or the path of a rivulet that funneled through the moss, Gretel began to feel better. Not less hungry or cold, but surer, more certain that they would survive. Which may be why it was she, and not Hansel, who finally called a halt to their wandering. "It is too dark to see," she told

her brother. "Let us find a cave or a hollow to keep out the wind. We can set out again at first light."

Hansel offered little argument and less help. After a few minutes, with no break in the dense trees, Gretel pointed to a great oak that lay across their path. "There be our cave," she said, walking around the fallen giant, noting with satisfaction the way the empty trunk opened into a small but dry chamber. While she gathered kindling for a fire and pine needles for their beds, her brother, as disconsolate as she had been earlier, blew on his fingertips and complained. "We will freeze before we starve. How thoughtful Stepmother was, to spare us a slow death for a quick one."

"There is no end of fuel for our fire," Gretel reassured him. Though she thought sadly of the tinderbox they kept by the hearth at home. "I will find some flint, and soon we shall have a blaze started."

Curled in the hollow of the tree beside her brother, Gretel fell quickly into an exhausted sleep. At first there was no angel in her dream, only a small house that lit up the woods around it. Surprised and delighted, she ran toward its shining windows and the curl of smoke like a friendly hand, beckoning. As she got closer, she was astonished to find that the cottage had been built with huge slabs of buttered gingerbread and dollops of meringue. There were two bushes by the door, one filled with lemon drops, the other with sugarplums. She thought she saw a figure in one

of the windows, though it could have been her own reflection, running eagerly toward the house.

But she reached neither the amber panes nor the sugarplums. Her angel, with a sorrowful countenance and Mama's long dark curls, suddenly barred the way. It shook its head and stamped its bare feet, then put out one hand and pointed a flaming fingertip at the girl's chest. Though she'd never resented her angel before, Gretel was confused now, even angry. As she woke to Hansel's shaking, she remembered the widespread wings and behind them the figure in the window, the bushes full of candy.

"Listen," her brother commanded, putting a rough hand over her mouth. "Only listen."

It was a bird's song, and if Gretel was surprised that Hansel even took notice of such a thing, she was more surprised by the song itself. The music wasn't human, though it sounded like someone singing under water, the words almost clear, nearly understood. She had no words, either, for the feelings the music stirred in her as she listened, though she recognized the pictures that danced in her head. The images she saw as the bird sang came straight from the dream she had just left: there was the house again, small and bright, and the figure in the window, waiting for her. And something else, something she couldn't see but was more real than all the rest. It was a mouthwatering smell, a smell that promised food she had never tasted, an unknown pleasure that drew her on like the ants she'd seen break ranks and swarm, madly, passionately, across a drop of honey.

Hansel must have been filled with the same images, the same scent. For together, without speaking, brother and sister rose and left the hollow of the tree. Side by side, they followed the bird's song to a nearby alder. The moment they reached the tree, though, the bird flew off and called to them from deeper in the forest. All morning they followed it, and as they walked, Gretel told her dream. With each detail she recalled, Hansel nodded, grinned. "Yes!" he said when she described the soft pink roof and the meringue that dripped from the eaves. "Exactly!" He even clapped his hands and slapped his knees when she told how the almond paste was carved into a door knocker and window boxes. "That's just how it is!" he told her.

When at last they came to a clearing and saw the house, Gretel stood frozen, remembering the way the angel had blocked her way. But Hansel raced for the dream. "Come on, girl!" he called, without looking back. "We are saved!"

The small swift—they could see it clearly now that it was out of the trees—that had led them here settled on the roof of the little cottage. It preened its feathers and was suddenly silent, as if to announce that its job was done, that there was no longer need for singing.

Hansel had already removed the marzipan door knocker and stuffed it into his mouth. Ravenous, he finished that and two sugarplums before he turned and scolded his sister. "Foolish thing!" he said. "Why do you stand there? Your angel sent you a dream of this good fortune." He laughed with unaccustomed

abandon, and pointed to the bird on the roof. "And her heavenly messenger has led us here."

But Gretel had not told him how the angel's finger still burned her chest. How she had actually checked under her shift to see if the skin was reddened there. It had not been, of course, and perhaps Hansel was right. Perhaps the angel had only meant that they should not take more than they needed, that they must repay the owner of the house for what they ate.

"We must knock," she told her brother. "We must offer to work for our food."

Hansel laughed again. "I have eaten the door knock, Gretel," he said, smiling like a naughty child, looking younger, lighter, and happier than she had ever seen him. "If we cannot knock, we shall sing for our supper, eh?" He came to her then and took her hand, wrapped his arm around her waist, and pulled her into a clumsy dance. Round and round he whirled her, singing the old song their father used to sing, until at last, giddy with his attention, she joined in:

"Oranges and lemons," say the bells of St. Clements.
"You owe me five farthings," say the bells of St. Martin.

For an instant, as they spun past the front window, Gretel thought she spied a shadowy figure staring out at them. She clasped one hand to her mouth, but as Hansel twirled them nearer, she saw that the window's glass was made of boiled sugar, cloudy and mottled as still water in a pond. Over its

surface, bobbing and weaving like falling leaves, were only their own silhouettes, their own dancing selves.

> *"When will you pay me?"* say the bells of Old Bailey.
> *"When I grow rich,"* say the bells of Shoreditch.
> *"When will that be?"* say the bells of Stepney.
> *"I do not know,"* says the great Bell of Bow.

But she could not mistake the voice that stopped their dance. That was real, as rasping and ugly as the swift's had been beautiful. "Nibble, nibble, little mouse." Hansel let go his sister's hand when he heard it. "Who is nibbling on my house?"

Too afraid to run, the children stood rooted to the spot. And again the crusty voice called to them from behind the very window where Gretel had dreamt shadows. "Perhaps 'tis the wind, heaven's child." The owner of the cottage laughed, but since the sound was closer to a growl, her paralyzed listeners were hardly reassured. "Only the wind, playful and mild."

When the door opened and a stooped crone with a halo of fine white hair appeared on the steps, Gretel and Hansel were both relieved. The old woman was a pathetic sight, after all, her thinning hair, her watery eyes, the stockings that fell in folds around her ankles. "Ay," she told them. "I was partly right, was I not? Two of heaven's children have found their way to my door."

"Good dame," Hansel began, using the same unctuous tone with which he addressed their stepmother when she was angry. "We only want . . ."

"I won't have it whispered about that I turned such inno-

cents into the woods." She smiled at them, though her mouth moved too slowly, too largely, as if it was unaccustomed to such an expression. "Well, come, then," she urged them, opening her door wide. "Out of the cold now, and I shall try to make us a bit of supper."

Supper was a feast—pancakes cooked on top of a brick oven that gave off a pleasant heat even when the hearth fire had died. The old woman served them cakes with nuts and fruit, and sweet cream that tumbled like a bountiful river from her china pitcher. The children, not trusting this sudden plenty, spoke little and ate a great deal. Then, bloated and easily won over by the promise of breakfast next morning, they followed the woman to a small room, where two beds covered with fresh white linens glowed like twin stars. They sank into a dreamless sleep, and neither could remember ever waking so late as they did next day.

Regaining some courage, and with it her manners, Gretel begged for work that might repay their elderly hostess's kindness. She could not help but notice the layers of dust beneath the stick candy on the walls and under the rush rug on the floor. "I might tidy the place a bit," she told the old woman, timidly. "I am fair handy, as well, with needle and thread."

"Do not trouble yourself," the woman told her. "There be only one small thing I need."

"Name it," said Hansel, sounding as though he was ready to perform miracles.

"'Tis something you might manage, young master," their hostess said. "Come and have a look at the wobbling leg on this chair." She led him back to the bedroom in which they'd passed the night, but when Gretel tried to come along, the woman pointed back to the kitchen. "There be the broom," she told the girl.

After she had swept the hearth, Gretel went in search of her brother. She tried the bedroom door and found it locked. "The young master must stay abed from now on," the old woman told her when she asked. "I shall not have him running off the lovely fat I plan to put on him."

Perhaps because Gretel had become accustomed to her stepmother's high-handed scorn, she was slow to apprehend the extent of the horror into which she and Hansel had stumbled. It took days of begging for scraps from the crone's table; of hearing the woman, whose voice no longer pretended any charity toward her at all, scold Gretel for drinking too much water or moving too slowly; of watching the witch (for what else could she be?) kneel and mumble prayers in a strange tongue before an altar covered with a blood-red cloth. It took the knife-sharp thorns of the black, bloomless brambles that had grown up around the house since she and her brother sought refuge there. And it took, finally, a chain of dreamless nights. Not once, after she had fallen, exhausted, into the brief sleep the witch allowed her, was Gretel visited by her winged guardian. It was a sign, she realized later, she should have taken to heart.

Eventually, though, she could delude herself no longer about the witch's plans. Three, and sometimes four times each day, the old woman took a brass key from around her neck and opened the door behind which Hansel now slept and ate. She always brought a tray with her heaped with elegant food: cakes and loaves and sugar tarts; cream and strawberries; even whole capons turned golden red on the spit above the kitchen fire. When she called Gretel to come get the dishes piled beside the door, the girl often heard the witch ask Hansel to hold out his hand. Through the keyhole, she watched the old woman circle his wrist with her gnarled fingers, and frown. "Not yet ready, my morsel," she would say, as if he were a roasting hen instead of a boy. "Not quite done."

It wasn't long before the witch, knowing Gretel would not leave her brother and that if she did there was no way out of the impenetrable thicket she'd contrived, began to treat the girl worse than ever. She fed her scraps, left her to sleep without a blanket, and at last grew as careless and talkative as if Gretel were a cat or dog, a pet that fended for itself but kept her company. "Ay," she grumbled one morning, stirring Hansel's porridge, "it has been a chain of long, lean days between meals. If I could eat such slop"—she stabbed at the pot with her spoon, then spat on the floor Gretel had swept only minutes before—"things would be different. But the blood thirst cannot be sated with your paltry human fare." She unhooked the cauldron from the hearth and set it to cool by the window. "'Tis a hunger to reckon with, a torture that feels close to madness when I must wait so long."

Gretel said nothing, knew the woman expected no reply. "But ah, when I feel that boy's flesh filling out, fat with life as he is of late, 'tis worth the pangs, the nights of waiting with my whole body crying out for him and my teeth rattling in my jaws."

Gretel knew, because the witch had told her, that if all went well, she would prepare her soulless feast soon. It was this fearful prospect that made the girl take a foolish risk and slip into Hansel's room the next time the old woman failed to lock the door. (The hungrier the crone got, the more forgetful she seemed. Once she even neglected to put on her shoes and clothes and spent the day naked, her wizened shins and third teat leaving Gretel torn miserably between laughter and tears.)

The room in which they'd spent that first night was much the same as Gretel remembered, except for the books and toys strewn everywhere. But in the midst of games and penny whistles, surrounded by whittled soldiers and chocolate candies, sat a boy she hardly recognized.

Hansel looked first at his sister's hands. "You have no tray," he said, his own hands describing a small, despairing arc in his lap. "I thought she might have sent you in her stead." Then he noticed her expression. "Why, girl, what is wrong? You look as though you see a haunt."

But it was no ghost Gretel stared at in disbelief. Her brother had far too much flesh on him to be a messenger from the other world. In fact, he was one of the stoutest people she had ever seen. In a few short months he had ballooned to twice his former size and lay propped on his pillows like a miniature pasha.

"You . . . you look . . . well fed." In fact, nothing that grew or walked or swam, nothing that Gretel could imagine, was meant to be so large. In a shameful moment, she even wondered how it was the witch could think her prize was not ready for the oven. "You must not eat any more, Brother." Hansel turned his cold, disapproving look on her, but she raced on, "Each bite you take puts you in greater danger. I hardly know how to tell you. The witch, she plans to—"

"Witch?" He looked even darker. "Mother is no witch. Though I suppose if she does not fancy you, she may seem so."

"'Mother'?" Gretel said the word aloud, and somehow speaking it herself was less horrible than hearing it on her brother's tongue. "'Mother'?"

"She has asked me to call her that, and so I shall if it pleases her." He leaned back, otiose, languid, and picked up a chocolate drop. He considered the candy, his expression almost fond, then popped it in his mouth.

"But how can you think she means you well?" Gretel was amazed that her brother had no idea what the crone was about. "We must run, Brother. We must leave here at once." She reached for one of his plump hands, but he pushed her away.

"Leave here?" Hansel sat up now, turning over a twig wagon filled with stone marbles. "Why should we leave someone who treats us with more kindness than our own parents?" He picked up a chapbook and opened it. "Why, she has even taught me to read." He lowered his head over the small volume. "This word is *raven*. See where it flies out of the pie?"

The more Hansel was content to sit and read, of course, the fatter he would grow. Gretel watched him pick up several more books, pointing proudly to pictures and to the single words that described them. "Even our own mother, girl, never taught us such wonders."

Gretel was fairly dancing with impatience. She had to convince Hansel of the danger they faced. And she had to do it before the old hag missed her. "You must understand. You must listen," she told him. "She feeds on human flesh."

"Ay." Hansel grinned ludicrously. "And this be a grand fellow I am eating, too." He pulled a gingerbread man from a chain of cookies strung beneath his window. Hugely, raucously, he chomped off its feet first, then its head.

"She means to eat you, too." There. Gretel had said it at last. She heard her own terrible words in the long silence that followed, that flowed like a thick current between them.

Until Hansel laughed. He even left off savaging the ginger man's body. He put his hands on his knees to steady himself, then rocked back and forth, roaring. The tears streamed from his eyes and down his newly dimpled cheeks. Back and forth, back and forth he rocked, until the room filled with his mirth and Gretel feared the witch would hear.

"Stop!" she commanded. "Stop and hear me." When he slowed a bit, she pushed her words in between the spasms of laughter. "Does she not feel your wrist each day?"

"Ay," he told her. "'Tis but to take my hand. She is wont to pat me often." He glared at his sister, but his tone was softer, al-

most a purr. "She cannot see at all well, Mother. She must touch where others look."

"She wants you fat enough to cook." Gretel was no longer careful how she put the matter. "When you are done, she will roast you in the oven."

But Hansel looked past her, or through her, she could not say which. "She has a right soft touch, Mother does," he said.

"She has told me!" Gretel stamped in frustration, tears in her eyes. "She has said it to me!"

Hansel no longer glared; his expression approached pity. "You are making it up," he told her. "Because she does not love you as she does me."

"'Love'!" Gretel was blinded by tears, by disbelief, by the word itself. How could he use such a word here, in this house? How could he use it about such a woman?

"She says I have nobility," he told her now. "When she sets eyes on me, 'tis as if she see a duke or a prince." His own fierce eyes fastened on Gretel again. "No one has ever looked upon me that way."

"But—"

"And you shall not take this from me for spite."

"It is not—"

"Go back to Father and our stepdame, if you wish." He almost rose from the bed, but perhaps his legs were not equal to the task of bearing his weight. He sank down to his bed again, sending more marbles across the floor. "As for me, I would rather die than go back to that thin gruel and those harsh words." If it

was not loyalty that shone in his eyes, it was at least pure contentment. "I shall not leave Mother."

Gretel despaired of changing his mind. Of saving his life. But still she took the twig from her pocket. "Take it," she told him. "If you give her this instead of your wrist—"

"Enough of your wiles, girl," he scolded. "Go back to the hearth."

"—she will think you have lost weight."

"Get out! Get out, before you ruin it all!"

"And she will feed you even more."

Her words found their mark. Gretel saw her brother stop, lean back on one round elbow, and consider. She plunged ahead, heaping him with delights. "Crumpets and pasties and those little blue eggs you like. Rabbit and trout and all manner of fowl."

He reached for the twig she proffered, reciting dreamily, "Pancakes and almond tarts, puddings and jam."

Gretel nodded. "More of everything," she agreed. "She will feed you twice, maybe three times as much as she does now."

When they heard the witch's shuffling footstep in the hall, Gretel had won only half what she'd hoped for: Hansel was delighted with the plan of tricking the old woman into feeding him more, a plan that, although he didn't know it, might spare his life. But she had still found no way to persuade him to leave that cursed house.

Gretel climbed out the bedroom window and circled back to the kitchen. The witch unlocked the door to visit her plump

cherub, unaware of the visitor who had left him seconds before. And so more weeks passed, and months as well, time that left Hansel plumper and Gretel and the witch more famished. For as the witch grew hungrier, she fed the girl less, too, and by the time she decided to put an end to her fast, neither of them could remember what a full stomach felt like. Gretel, as she lay by the hearth at night, her poor insides churning and empty, remembered the way Mother, at the end, would push away the trays Gretel brought. *I will have none of that,* she'd say. *Just sing me another song, sweet. 'Tis that will fill me up.* And sometimes it was enough to put her to sleep, humming the old song, the lullaby Mama craved.

"There be no use," the witch said one day, as Gretel had known she must. The crone threw her book of spells at Gretel, though it fell short of its mark and skittered along the floor. "I have prayed and chanted and fed the boy until I am worn with toil." She waved a frail hand at the girl. "I may as well eat a skinny thing like you."

She rose then and, with a horrible finality, walked to the drawer where she kept her knives and skewers. "I have conjured cornmeal and compotes, peacock and ham hocks. I have summoned up soups and stews. Soufflés and crab cakes. But still he loses flesh." She sharpened one of her longest, cruelest knives on a whetstone, brushing it faster and faster across the oiled rock. "I have coddled and spoiled him and emptied his foul pan."

She held up the gleaming knife now and, before Gretel could

pull away, sliced off a lock of the girl's hair. "Sharp enough to do the job," she said, grinning at the curl of fine hair in her hand. "I will have him this day. I can wait no longer."

But when she led him to the table and bade him wait while she stoked the fire, even when the oven got so hot they could feel it across the room, Hansel did not fear the witch. He sat, his haunches overflowing the small bench beside the trestle, and smiled. "What treat shall we have tonight, Mother?" he asked. "It must be a feast if you cannot carry it on a tray." He gripped his spoon and knife, as if the food were already in front of him.

Did he call the crone Mother to please her? Gretel wondered. Or did he nurse some dark angel of his own—the image of a mother made of yams and comfits, chops and pies?

"There shall be no feast until I can make this oven hot enough, my lamb," the witch told him. "Perhaps you could come see if the flue is blocked." She gestured toward the fiery oven. "This old frame is too stiff to bend so low."

If her frame was too old, the boy's was surely too broad. But he stood with what alacrity he could muster and went to her side. "Let me see, Mother," he said, bending down, peering into the blood-red innards of the stove.

Just as Gretel dreaded, the witch rushed at her brother, a look of such fierce yearning on her face that for a moment the girl stood paralyzed. But then, just in time, she reached out and pulled her brother away from the stove, and what had started could not be stopped. The old woman, hands outstretched to

push her boy-roast in the oven, fell into the flames herself. The children watched in horror as, blind with agony, the witch crawled deeper into the fire instead of finding the way out. Hansel put his hands in to reach her, but the witch, in her anguish, writhed out of his grasp. "Fools! Fools!" she wailed as the smoke and heat did their work. Once more Hansel reached into the flames, and once more failed to catch hold of the witch before the fire forced him back. "Fools! Fools!" And then her mouth was lost, her skin, her need to cry out at all.

There was silence, blessed silence until Gretel noticed her brother's hands. "Here," she said tenderly, reaching for his burned fingers. "Let me get some salve."

But Hansel pulled away from her. "No!" he screamed. "Do not touch me. Do not dare touch me."

"But your hands are terribly burnt." Gretel looked up from her brother's hands to his face, and lost her breath. What she saw there was hate, burning and bottomless.

"You killed her!" Hansel's skinless hands were balled into fists, and he was crying as she had never seen him cry before.

"But Brother," she said, "she would have pushed you in." She backed away from his eyes, for they seemed to give off a heat like the oven's.

"You were jealous!" he screamed at her, anger turning his round cheeks pink as beef fillets. "It was you she kept working and me she fed."

Gretel backed toward the stove, which still smelled of burn-

ing flesh and sulfur. "You couldn't stand to see one of us safe and happy and protected," he yelled. "Only one of us, sister mine. That was it, wasn't it? Only one!"

"Of course not," she told him, hearing herself whimper, trying to escape those eyes even as the heat from the oven grew behind her.

"You wanted to drag me back home." He was no longer screaming but spoke as slowly, harshly, as a wheel turning on cobbles. "You wanted me to be poor again, to drink soup made of water."

The stove's flames, fed by the witch, leapt higher now and Gretel tried to move toward Hansel. But he pushed her back. "Mother loved me more than anyone ever has"—slowly, relentlessly, he advanced toward her—"but you could not bear it, could you?"

"No! Surely, you know—"

"I know that your mewling angel never fed us as Mother did." He bore down on her, raw hands shaking, his face filled with rage and tears. "I know that no one will ever care for me as she did."

And then he was on her, but not before someone else barred the way. Gretel's angel, sudden, soundless, stood between brother and sister. Just as the boy tried to push Gretel backwards into the flames, the angel with their mother's face stopped him. A white-hot light surrounded it, steamed off the milk-white shoulders and wings. The finger it pointed at the boy, Gretel knew, was molten. It touched Hansel lightly on the chest and

he screamed in pain. For a minute he hesitated, but, staring right through the angel, glaring at Gretel, he charged again. Growling with fury, he hurled himself at her, and if her angel had not pulled her away, it would have been the end of her. Instead, it swept Gretel up, as if they were dancing, and whirled her away, while Hansel raced headlong, screaming, into the flames.

When she set out for home, Gretel took some of the witch's cooking pots and a basket of food that would only go to mold if she left it behind. She could not carry more because her hands still ached from the flames she had braved at the end. When her brother fell into the oven, she had tried to pull him out. With no more thought to her own safety than a loyal dog protecting its master, she had leaned against the poker-hot opening of the stove and reached into the fire. But the searing pain, the breath-less heat, brought her to her senses. She pulled back and watched in horror as Hansel rushed to his make-believe mother, as he picked up the flaming husk that had been the witch. As the skin ran like melting wax from his arms, he crumpled to the oven floor and raised his hands above his head as if surrendering to the roaring tongues that devoured him, bit by bit.

The thorny brambles had dissolved as soon as the witch died, and Gretel now made her way easily back into the woods through which she and Hansel had wandered before the old woman had trapped them. As she walked, the girl found ivy and chickweed to make poultices for her hands and for the bright red

scar that crossed her waist where she'd leaned against the stove. Though she had no idea how far or which direction she and her brother had traveled, she was not afraid. Each night her angel leaned over her dreams, kissed her burning hands, and whispered the way to take next morning. By the time she reached her father's house, spring was coming on; tender shoots curled out of the ground, and birds flew once more in packs so thick they peppered the sky.

The old man, for old he suddenly seemed, was outside chopping wood as Gretel came up the rise toward the cottage. When he saw her, he dropped his ax and went mad with joy. "Gret, Gret!" he called, folding her to him, making the pots she carried clank and clatter. "You are home. You have come home at last!"

When she shrank back, peering toward the dark cottage, he shook his head. "You have naught to fear, child," he told her. "Your stepdame fetched poison berries from a fair on St. Joseph's Day. They gave me a fearsome bellyache, but they stole the life clean out of her."

"She is dead, then?" Gretel had seen enough death of late; the news gave her little joy.

"Ay," her father told her, linking his arm through hers, leaning on her as he had never done before she left. "But let us talk of pleasant stuff. There be time enough for sorrow." He led her to the door of the house, then looked behind her, toward the rise she had just climbed. "Say where your brother is and when he will join us here."

The time for sorrow came sooner than he must have hoped.

For Gretel told him how brother and sister had found the witch's house but only one of them had left it behind. She told him about her angel, and how it had saved her from the fire that killed both the old crone and Hansel. It was clear, though, from the way her father listened to the tale, the way he held his head in his hands, that he did not believe her.

"I tried to save him, Da. Truly, I did." But when Gretel held up her hands as proof, she saw how her angel's kisses had healed them, how they looked as white and smooth as if she had worn gloves along her rough and tangled way.

Father's eyes, the way they fell from hers, told her what he thought. "Hunger can drive God's love from our hearts," he said. "It can turn us into beasts." He stood beside Gretel, staring at the empty, sloping hills. "When times were still hard, not two days after we left you lambs in the woods, your stepmother tried to steal a crust from me. She came at me while I slept, slipped her hand into my pocket like a thief. Taken sudden that way, I struck her hard across the mouth.

"Whatever you did, child, is less than some and more than others. It's done and forgotten." There was weariness in his voice, and a dim gratitude. "The witch was starving you, but you have come home with food." At last he raised his eyes to hers. "You have come home with that slow smile of your ma's."

He reached for his daughter's hand. "We will tell the neighbors you have both returned." Gretel heard the surrender, the tired truce behind his words. "I have been without family for too

long. I shall not lose you to sheriff's men, to a tribunal and the noose."

So her father shaped a new story, with a happy ending, repeating it again and again—to neighbors and peddlers and travelers; to brides and housewives who began afresh, now that the drought was passed, to pay for Gretel's handiwork and lace. *Once upon a time,* it seemed, *there were two children, a boy and a girl.* Father told of the witch, the gingerbread, and the oven. He told of the fire and the way the witch had planned to fatten the boy. He described with pride how his children had tricked her, how they had come home to him, hand in hand. "Of course, you know the way of young men," he always added at the end. "No sooner does Hansel come home than he takes a fancy to a comely lass from Wainridge. He is off courting, but my girl is home to stay."

Each time her father told the lie, Gretel felt as if he had branded her. The mark of Cain burned on her forehead, turning her awkward and ashamed in front of others. She had tried to save her brother, but only she and her angel had seen it. And perhaps God. What wouldn't she give to trade her heavenly father's trust for her earthly one's!

But she knew her da was right. She would never leave him now. Where was there to go? Where could she hide from the memory of Hansel racing into the fire? From the foolish, useless wish that she had said enough, done enough, been enough to save him?

So she stayed. Her father needed her, after all. Her table linens and scarves helped put food on their table. And if he blamed her for her brother's death, he never said so outright. Only sometimes she caught a look on his face, a shadow when she looked up from her sewing and found his eyes on her. It wasn't like the hate she had seen on Hansel's; she could never have lived with that. It was more like pity. Though pity for her or himself, she could not have said.

It did not matter. She had her angel. She could endure the cold stream where she took their buckets each morning. And the endless succession of days, like heavy, rough-scaled logs across her back—she could survive that, too. She could bear the mark Da's stories set on her forehead, because every night, in her dreams, it was kissed away. She worried sometimes, as she waited by the hearth for sleep to come, that it might not happen, that the angel might fail her. But it never did. Night after night, even after her father had died and Gretel was an old woman who lived by herself, the sweet moment always returned.

Once she had drifted past thought, Gretel found herself again in the woods. Again she stood by the small house trimmed with delights. But this time she walked without fear to the open door and the figure that waited there. Sweeter than a lemon drop, softer than caramel was the kiss Gretel's angel placed on her forehead. And when she was once more folded into the milk-white arms, Gretel felt no mark, no shame, only a tide of joy that rushed to fill her head, her heart, her whole body. Like a flood

of music bursting from a small bird's chest, love forced itself through her bones and skin and erupted in a single perfect flower. *Mother,* she said as she held the angel fast. *Mother,* she sighed as she rested her head on the creamy shoulder. *Mother,* as the two of them turned their backs on the world and walked to-gether until dawn.

Ashes

Even a young prince can be jaded. I had endured countless receptions and balls, had watched an endless parade of aristocratic beauties present themselves for my approval—and for secret embraces in shadowed chambers or damp-walled gardens (giggling, rustling skirts, and then the sun too bright on a painted cheek). But this lost, thin-waisted nymphet was different. My mother noticed it first.

"Did you see that girl?" The queen stood beside me at the top of the stairs and studied the ballroom below us. "The one with Sir Lewis." Only a second before she had dismissed the gaggle of dancers, turned her back on the view from the balcony, and snapped open a perfumed fan pulled from her sleeve. Now, though, her eyes narrowed with interest, and she leaned over the railing. Like colorful gems spilled from a purse, men and women in velvet and satin moved across the marble tiles, each couple following the pattern of the pair in front of them.

"Look! She's charmed the old fool into a gavotte. It's a wonder he can hoist that monstrous frame out of bed in the morning, much less drag it about to a jig."

I glanced idly at the ragged chain of dancers beneath me. It was hard to miss chubby Lewis—bobbing up and down to his own private music while the others kept proper time—but once I had spotted the old fellow, I could not take my eyes from his partner. It was not the blue dress or the crystal slippers that shed rainbows as she twirled. It was not the lace gloves or the tiny jeweled bows that winked from her train. It was the way she carried herself—or, more accurately, the way she didn't. Instead of posing, doll-like, she floated, spinning and turning like a leaf, from hand to hand.

The queen, still focused on the great hall spread below us, must have noticed my interest. "I am glad," she told me, without taking her eyes from the pageant of the dance, "you are not like some, mongrels led here and there, driven only by their base appetites." I barely listened, already dizzied by the whirling fairy below me. "Perhaps your refusal to wed has been well advised, my son. Perhaps it will secure you now a bride of a different sort."

After I had kissed my mother's cheek and worked my way to the bottom of the stairs, the fairy dancer was my reward. As glowing and impartial as the sun, she took my arm for the next carole with the same smile she gave poor Lewis in farewell. She seemed, in fact, to have no idea who I was.

"You make the old dances seem new," I told her. "How has grace and beauty like yours stayed hidden from our court?" Something in her countenance unmanned me. The blaze of sconces twinkled behind her, and my flattery seemed empty and foolish.

"I have never been to court," she told me, training curious,

unblinking eyes on mine. "Or danced like this, or met anyone like you."

"Surely I am not so different from other men." I laughed, more confident now. This was a game I had played before, over and over until I knew the script by heart, all the blushes, every whispered lie.

"Perhaps not," she replied. "But except for my father and the kind gentleman who danced with me just now, you are the only man I have ever spoken to." She cocked her head like a pretty sparrow and studied me while we spun. "You are so tall and fair, you quite take my breath away!"

She should have colored and curtsied; she should have lowered her gaze from mine. But her eyes, wide and greedy, devoured my face, and she laughed like a man, her head held back, her mouth unhidden by her hands.

I searched the weary catalogue of women I had known. Not one of them had looked like this, had danced like this, had stirred to life an open rush of affection I thought had died years before.

I learned the games early, you see. My first memory is of the endless carpet, the long trail along which my nurse led me to the tall, lovely woman who sat with her maids and laughed like music. "Mother, look what I have made for you," I cried, dropping my chain of dandelions in her lap, trying to scramble after them.

But the laughter stopped and the beautiful woman frowned. "Now look what the child has done! There is dirt all over my dress. Hannah! Hannah, come get him, quick."

As I spun around the floor with this sweet stranger, the years

fell away and it seemed a child, trembling with adoration, had laid a chain of flowers in *my* lap. I stared at the girl in my arms and wondered if love was this simple.

"You cannot be a prince!" She laughed when I told her who I was. Her honeyed hair shook free from the combs that held it, and her hands, as if forgotten, rested in mine. "You are much too young and you do not scare me at all. Why, if you were not so important, we should be real friends!"

I forgot the lessons my mother and all the powdered ladies of the court had taught me. I neglected to bow and lie in wait, to flatter and pretend. "We are already friends," I told her. When the music started up again, I whirled us into a shadowy alcove, away from prying eyes. "Now tell me your name, sweet friend."

She stopped dancing and pulled me to a cluster of pillars at the edge of the hall. There she leaned against the sugared stone and whispered to me as if she were at confession. "I am afraid I no longer have a name of my own. After my father died, my step-mother called me nothing but Cinderella." She seemed as small and frightened as a bird I dared not flush. "I have not led an easy life."

"Your mother must have been very beautiful." It was an old formula, but I said it with new sincerity. She clung to the pillar, though, as if I had set a snare for her.

"I suppose she must," she said without affectation. "My father always said she was. But I cannot remember her face." And when she turned back to me at last, her eyes were filled with a strange and cloudy hunger I dreamed suddenly of feeding.

"When I was little and had no one to run to if I fell and hurt myself, no one to share the games I played alone among the mops and kettles, I used to try to picture her. I cried and yearned and prayed, but I could never see her eyes, her hair, not so much as the tips of her fingers."

She studied her own small hands in silence, then raised a face to which the light had rushed back. "So I have made up my own mother." She grinned like a clever child. "She is a fairy god-mother, more radiant and powerful than anyone on earth. I can-not hold or kiss her, but she protects me with her spells."

She spoke as if she were still in a nursery. I laughed now, en-chanted, and bent to kiss her. When she turned away once more, I was not angry but patient and tender. "And why not have kisses as well as spells?" I asked. "Surely a woman's dreams em-brace more than elves and fairies?"

She did not leave the shelter of the pillar, only looked at me from its shadow. "Perhaps they do," she told me. "I used to see my godmother as clearly as I see you. She came to me in the day-time, real as the corn, bright as dawn on a stream. Now she vis-its only after dark, when there is no light to see how she wears her hair or the color of her dress." She squeezed my hand tightly, and her voice rose, colored with hope. "But last night was differ-ent. She came to me, really and truly. She promised me you."

Though her face and manner held me in thrall, I could make little sense of her childish words. I took them for flattery and fell into the easy habit of flirtation. "Promises," I told her, bowing gallantly, "must not be broken." With that, I took her arm and

whirled her deeper into the alcove we'd found under the arch of the marble stairs. We danced on, just the two of us, plotting like runaways, smuggling in morsels from the banquet table. We formed our own tiny kingdom there, like the make-believe land I used to inhabit when my mother and father fought.

Before he died, the king had vanquished thousands of enemy troops but never won a single confrontation with his queen. As my mother's voice rose higher, spiraling toward outrage and anguish, the servants would shake their heads and Father would retreat to his chambers, apologizing, begging forgiveness all the way down the hall.

While these battles royal raged, I would hide under these very same stairs, my hands against my ears. If I closed my eyes, I could travel far away from the yelling and from the dark, intricate oaths issuing from my father's rooms. But of course, such respites never last. Neither did my time with the fairy dancer, Cinderella.

Too soon, I saw her grow restless, watched her count from our sanctuary the guests who had begun to drift in laughing clusters toward the door. Then, high in the castle tower, above the gods and goddesses painted on the ceiling, a bell began to ring midnight. Stricken, Cinderella looked up the marble stairs toward the guards at the door. "I must go!" She grabbed her train, darted back into the sea of silk and satin from which I had plucked her, and disappeared.

"Wait!" Midnight tolled again, and my mother, determined but unhurried, moved toward me down the stairs. "You did not

tell me your family's name!" I saw a small figure gliding like a skater across the field of gold and marble, then gave chase. "How will I know where to find you?"

Too late, I pushed my way through the crowd, brushed past my mother, and reached the door. I raged at the watchmen who had let her climb into the silver coach that clattered out the gate as the last stroke of midnight hammered against the sky.

One of the watchmen, a burly fellow big enough to break me in two if I had not been his prince, hung his head, ashamed, while the other two pointed to a lost star that lay glittering in the moonlight on the bottom step.

The queen followed me down the stairs and leaned over the star burning my palm. "In order to wear that shoe, one would have to be a fairy or a child," she decided, straightening. "If she is the first, you will never see her again. But if you danced this night with a human, I swear we will ferret her out."

They made a joke of the story. In the streets and markets, they laughed at the love-struck prince who sent soldiers to every town. Who had his hopes raised and dashed a thousand times before he finally found his commoner sweetheart in a merchant's kitchen beside the grate, her elbows sooty and her hair filled with ashes.

Of course, the wags made much of the fact that it was a house my father had once frequented. They took relish in reviving old

scandals and the foolish boasts of a widow in the habit of brag-
ging about her "connections" to the palace. But those gossips
never saw the smile with which Cinderella ran to me that day.
They did not hear her laugh, warm and triumphant, as I placed
the glass slipper on her foot. "My friend," I told her, "I was not
certain I would ever be this happy again."

"And I?" she replied, brushing away the soot that clung to my
sleeve. "I knew I would. If not, I should have died." Now she
opened her arms and I scooped her from the hearth. Her fawn-
ing sisters bobbed up and down, bowing and crying as I helped
her to my horse. Her stepmother stood bemused, then waved as
if she had planned it all. She smiled at last, urging her daughters
and her neighbors to bid us farewell as we raced like children to
our palace of dreams.

Not without cost. The fact that my sweetheart's father had
been, before he died, a wealthy man did little to stop busy tongues.
Like a poison that infected the court and the market alike, talk of
"Cinderella, the barefoot princess" spread everywhere. Old wives
giggled over their stewpots, and ladies in waiting whispered at
their sewing. They chattered and cackled and chewed on the story
as though it were a meaty bone. How she had won a prince's
heart, how she had cast a spell and caught a kingdom. Yet my
mother, who usually despised such gossip, seemed not to mind.

"This foolish prattle will pass," she told me one morning. She
had taken, since I'd brought home my future wife, to summoning
me every day to her chambers, to looking more flushed and eager

as the marriage date drew near. It was as if she, not Cinderella, were to be wed. "Before your father died, there were rumors, too. The people love to think their rulers fall in love with commoners. It is nothing—all idle, empty talk."

I had heard the gossip myself, the tired legend of my father's dalliances, his fondness for castle servants, tavern wenches, and finally a certain comely widow whose company he enjoyed until the queen's soldiers visited her home and persuaded her it was best to foreswear royal companionship. Though the king had died more than a dozen years before, this perverse legacy lived on. It was, in fact, nearly all I had left of him. I was only a lad of four, after all, when the great bells pealed all night and my mother took to her bed. I cried then, kicking my toy soldiers from their orderly phalanxes and burying them deep in the furthest corner of the kitchen garden. Now, though, I could barely remember the face of the man whose death had made a kingdom weep.

"Our subjects will have other things to occupy their idle tongues once you take the throne, my son. When your father's bloodline is assured, there will be no stopping us. Armies will be mustered; taxes will be raised. We will live as our birthrights demand."

I considered the balls, the jewels, the damask tablecloths and mirrored halls. "We already live beyond most people's dreams," I told her. "What more could you want?"

The queen's maids sat around her that day, two whispering over a tapestry, one plucking softly at a mandolin. My mother, who had been sewing as she spoke, stood suddenly, showering

the floor with brocade and ribbon. "I have waited a long time for what your marriage will bring," she told me. Her fervor, her eagerness, filled her face with light and made it younger than her years.

"And when, may I ask, am I to meet the princess apparent?" She sat again, her servants hastening to pick up the tumbled ribbons and lay them in her lap. She sighed then, her eyes closed and one ringed hand on her breast. "Am I not to see for myself the treasure you have wrested from its hiding place?"

I sat beside her. "You know very well that Cinderella and I have come to visit you every day. But you have been busy with your maids or else in your bath."

It was an old trick of hers, making me wait. I recalled running to her chambers, as a boy, with some urgent news, some childish triumph. I would stand outside that intricate, sweet-smelling realm of hers, slices of laughter fluttering out to me whenever the door opened. Like an exile from the promised land, I yearned to be let in. Sometimes it was days and days between my glimpses of her, so that at last nothing seemed as important, nothing as wondrous, as what I had been denied.

It was not until the wedding day that my wife and my mother met face-to-face. In the interim, my sweetheart and I walked in the garden, took rides in the woods, though all along I sensed that my orphaned darling, just like the motherless boy I had once been, was waiting only to meet the queen. Finally, to my sweet

relief, the bells rang, our carriages lined up for the ride to church, and the horses stamped, their breath smoky in the morning air. The queen, decked in fur, put her white hand into my bride's and smiled thinly. The new princess, unschooled in subtlety, missed the condescension that set my mother's face as if it were carved. All Cinderella saw, to judge from the admiration that shone in her eyes, was a dark-haired beauty who burned like a cool taper beside her own bright flame.

And flame she did. Her dress was white silk lined with ermine, picked by my mother for its icy elegance. But my sunny love outshone her chaste gown, as lovely a bride as any dream could conjure. All the way to church, waving to the crowds from our velvet nest, the people's "barefoot princess" trailed beauty like streamers as crowds of goggle-eyed children chased our carriage down the street. Later, as we spoke the marriage pledges, our words trembling doves in the dark chapel, I watched tears trace her cheeks and melt into her smile.

That night, all the cruel gossip seemed forgotten. It was a small price to pay, as at last I led Cinderella to a candlelit room and closed the door. I took her hand and stooped to blow out the light beside our bridal bed. But her hand and her voice stopped me. "No, please. I can't see how lovely it is in the dark."

I shook my head, but obliged her. Then, with all the yearning that I had learned to stifle, with all the love I had saved, I untied her bodice and bent to kiss the brand-new face of love. She lifted her mouth to mine, but pulled back as I tried to unlace the shift

that covered her breasts. "Do not take it off just yet," she said. "Let us dance first, you and I." She held her slender arms out to me and looked so like a child begging one more sweet that I walked into her embrace and held her fast. We whirled around the room while she sang off-key an old peasant song I had not heard in years.

"This is the way it was the night we met," she told me. "The magic felt just like this. The lights were shining, and you looked at me with just those eyes. Tell me what you saw."

"I saw my dream," I said. "I saw the fairest, most wondrous creature that ever walked the earth." She laughed, tossing her head and letting me slip my hand beneath the shift. "I saw a princess dressed in light, a fairy sporting moonbeams in her hair."

I laid her on the bed and began to kiss away the shift. Still she stopped me, begging for another dance. "Tell me how it was. How the magic made me look."

I could hardly speak for the knot of longing in my throat. But I held her gently, wooed her with tenderness and a patience born of years. "You looked as you do now." I touched her under the frothy gown she could not bear to part with. There would be time, I thought, for wearing away this shyness. Long chains of days together, filled with growing ease and love. She fell into the cloud of linens around us and her arms circled my neck. "As fair as any woman I hope to know."

When I woke my bride was gone and a single streak of sun shot across the floor and up the sheets. Once I had stowed the chamber pot and made my way to the window, the world seemed fresher, more promising than I had ever seen it. The trees trembled with excitement and every hill sloped toward some undiscovered joy. I dressed quickly, eager to find Cinderella, to spend our first day in the sweet intimacy I had nursed in my imagination for weeks.

I heard them laughing as I passed my mother's chambers. The sound stopped me in the cold hallway and drew me to the door. It was swung wide and I could see most of the sitting room from where I stood. A tiny tremor, not as sharp as disappointment, kept me on the threshold, watching the women at my mother's feet. They were clustered on pillows and footstools, some sewing, others working on the hair of the fair-headed beauty at the queen's knee. Her laugh was the gayest of all, as they fussed and giggled, rearranging combs and braiding tresses. "Is this the style you meant, Mother?" my sweetheart asked, turning to face the queen, then bringing a nervous hand to a curl that had strayed from its place. "Is it really French?"

My mother looked down from her perch above them. Her inspection was thorough and emotionless. "Exactly," she concluded at last. "It's perfect for you, my dear." There was a hint of a smile on her face, until she glanced up and saw me at the door. All the women followed her gaze, staring blankly, as if I were a curious menagerie specimen that had somehow wandered into their human society.

In that instant, something ancient and dispiriting gripped me, but I shook it off. When the frozen tableau spilled into action, bits of silk flying, a gilded mirror winking its bright eye at the ceiling, all the women rose and my mother walked to meet me. She stopped me just inside the door, and turned her face aside to be kissed.

Behind her trailed my Cinderella, flushed and self-conscious in her new coiffure. Again she touched a loose feather of hair. "Your mother has been showing me how they dress in the French court," she told me over the queen's shoulder. "Do you like it?"

I hardly heard her question. Her presence in my mother's chamber, her wild hair caught up in a stylish prison, disconcerted me. "I woke just now," I said, ignoring my mother's cheek and the ring of rustling skirts around me, "and you were gone."

She laughed nervously. "I am afraid I shall never be a stay-abed princess. I was up with the birds, and your mother was kind enough to send for me." She withdrew further behind the queen, deferential and shy, but her eyes swam with secret, hidden delight.

"Well, now that you are abroad," my mother announced, "your new bride is at your disposal. All that remains is to secure her Parisian look with a pin or two. Then she will join you in the garden." She moved forward, forcing me to step backwards out of the room. "Surely," she said, smiling at the women around her, "a prince's passions can be reined for fashion's sake." She nodded at one of the women who reached for the door. "And

French fashion at that!" As they were shut away from me, I heard the laughter start up again and saw my princess giggling with the rest, one hand raised delicately to hide her mouth.

She spent most of that day with the queen. She stole back to me between her lessons in royalty, rushing to share each fresh marvel, each trinket or mannerism that removed her further and further from the sweet openness with which I had fallen in love. When dinner was over and night pried her from my mother's side, I proposed a different sort of lesson.

"Let us ride tomorrow, just the two of us," I said. "I know a stream that will take us far from courtly courtesies and gossip. A place made for whispers and long embraces."

"Oh, no, we cannot," she told me, alarmed. "We must not. Your mother has arranged for three of her finest seamstresses to fit me tomorrow. Besides, why on earth would we want to leave the castle?" Her question stung only a little, a tiny prick like a spring bumblebee's. "Who would ever want to leave such happiness?"

"My love, your heart and not your eyes should tell you where happiness lies." I took her in my arms, remembering the night we had met, the way she had laughed without affectation, had looked at me with the steady, direct gaze of a child. "Surely you know that gowns and perfumed lace conceal and deceive? Sweep them away, toss them aside, and there is truth."

She pulled back from me, her sparkle turned hard. "'Sweep them away'?" Her lips pursed as if she had tasted something bitter beyond words. "'Toss them aside'? Who are you to preach simplicity? I have done without your sweet deceptions my whole life, while you were playing at draughts and bending your knee to nothing more demanding than a dance tune!"

"My dear bride," I told her. "My mother is full of beguilements, but you must—"

"I dreamt of your despised courtesies while I lived a life of truth and ashes. Your gowns and your gossip kept me alive and warm with desire." She walked to the window, pulled back the curtain, and stared at the garden, frosted with moonlight. "Sweep them away? I would sooner die!"

Her back was as straight and narrow as a flame. From the bed, I spoke to that small, imperious spine. "Can you not see what the queen is doing?" I asked. "She wants to mold you, change you." Impossibly, her back grew straighter still. "She wants to put out your spark, to leave you cold and false. My love, you are to be a mirror in which she sees herself."

Cinderella let the drape fall back, pale fists at her sides. "I hope she *can* mold me! I pray she will!" She moved forward like a sleepwalker, her voice low, her eyes misted, unfocused. "When I lay by the hearth without a mother or father to warm me, when I scrubbed and slopped and hoed, when my hands and feet turned raw from the cold of the barn, I dreamt of a beautiful woman who would love me."

"But dearest—"

"And now I have found her at last. Your mother looks precisely like the fairy guardian I conjured out of loneliness and hurt. She has come back to me, more beautiful even than my childish hopes."

"Is it not time, my love, to put away your godmother's imaginary spells? To give up these sad old dreams?" I led her to the mirror beside our bed. I turned her to face the two of us in its glass. "Here is your present and your future. Here is your new life."

She studied our reflections, but her eyes seemed to peer deep inside the glass, behind my consternation, past her own loveliness. "'Old'? 'Sad'?" she said, mocking me. "Sad enough to turn a house wench into a princess! Old enough to make a queen my mother! A mother who will stay with me always, just as I dreamt."

"*I* am with you, too." My tone was petulant; even I heard the small boy's whine behind my words. *(I am sorry I made you unhappy, Mama. I have been so lonely without you.)* Perhaps moved by my pitiable tone, Cinderella came to bed then, sat beside me while I unbuttoned her jeweled vest. Like an obedient pet, she allowed me to undress her until I tried to slip away the long layers of petticoat that rustled around us.

"Wait," she begged as before, her eyes staring so deeply into mine, I thought she had found a new mirror there. "Tell me how it was that night. How you fell in love with a fairy princess. How she danced and whirled and stole your heart away."

When a kitten slips its head beneath your hand, it is little

enough trouble to pet it, to stroke the soft head and back until it purrs. She required only a few words, a memory that pleased us both. So I told her again how she shone at the ball. How no eyes could look away from the lovely dancer, how the hours were like minutes as the blue satin swept round the room and the glass slippers spun webs of light across the floor.

As I recited the litany, she held me tight, her nails digging through my shirt. Each time I paused, she pulled away and held me at arm's length, laughing. "More!" she demanded, tossing her head like a spoiled child. "Tell me more!" And like a doting fool with a pretty changeling on his lap, I helped her see it all again: the grand hall lined with glittering torches, the tapestried walls, the carved satyrs holding up a painted sky. And at the center of it all, whirling like a firefly, a fragile golden girl catching us in her spell.

My hands under the petticoats, I retold the rings that had sparkled through her lace gloves. Against her ear, her neck, her damp white breast, I whispered of the satin bows at which the queen had stared in fascination from her balustrade decked with flowers. When the story was done, Cinderella sighed softly and drew me to her.

I woke again to an empty bed. Sweating, I rolled away from the stream of sun that striped the pillow, dressed hurriedly, and went in search of my bride. There was no one in the queen's chambers but an aged servant who had been ordered to wait for me. "They

are in the east garden," she told me over her sewing. "They re-
quest you to join them there."

Fussing with roses and chattering amid stalks of lilies, my
wife and mother looked up with mild annoyance when I arrived.
"Oh, good. You're here at last." While she spoke, the queen advanced on the lilies, cutting blooms with a precise and practiced
hand. The huge white heads dropped one by one into a basket
held by the princess beside her. "We have a boon to ask, have we
not, my dear?"

A small rose the color of egg yolk peeked from my wife's hair.
"Yes," she said, smiling uncertainly into my mother's steely eyes.
I had to laugh now at my foolish fear that the queen could mold
Cinderella into an image of herself. Standing together, the two
could not have looked more different. One was dark and stately,
with a sharpness that had already hardened her beauty. The
other was fair and changeable as sunlight, as innocent as a new
day. "That is, your mother thought, and so did I . . ."

"It would be a wedding gift," my mother finished for her. "A
way of announcing your choice to all the world." She bent to
snip a calla, then stood again, the silver shears flashing. "A way,
too, of putting an end to vicious talk and preserving honor in the
wake of your somewhat hasty match."

I knew the talk of Princess Cinders was painful, not only to
the queen, but to my love as well. "Worthy goals all," I admitted
warily. "But why are the means so long in coming?"

The queen turned to cut another flower while my sweetheart
raced to place the basket by her side. "Not long at all," Mother

announced, "provided a little decisiveness can be mustered to un-
dertake a somewhat distasteful task."

"Such as?"

She faced me now, forcing the princess to scurry to her other
side. "We want your bride's stepmother and sisters executed."

I could hardly believe my ears. I searched Cinderella's face for
a trace of the horror I felt myself. But in the countenance she
raised to the queen's, I saw only adoration. "Three lives lost for
honor's sake?" I could not hide my outrage. "What sort of honor
is it, Mother, that requires human sacrifice?" The basket of lilies
dipped as I raised my voice, the ponderous heads rolling around
its rim. "If honor breeds such schemes, I would hate to see the
work of knaves."

"Is it knavish, then, to right wrongs?" The queen, hooking
her shears to a chain around her waist, bore down on me, and
the princess backed away. "To avenge the trials and strife your
wife has undergone?"

"Those are avenged in her every day with me." I stepped to
my bride, forcing her to face me and look into my eyes. "My
friend," I told her, "you are my princess and my wife. Do you
need to draw blood in confirmation of our love?"

Like the sun drawn to the earth, my wife's eyes left mine and
sought support in my mother's tranquil smile. "I—I only want
to know that love is stronger than fear, that those horrible
women can never hurt me again.

"Last night while you were sleeping, I thought I woke beside
the grate again, covered with ashes. My eyes were filled with

smoke and my head ached from the names they had hurled at me like stones." She lowered her head now, and her voice dropped to a whisper. "'Cinderella' was the least of them. I cannot tell the rest."

I took the basket from her and would have put my arms around her, but the queen drew her aside. "You shall not suffer so again," she said, an overblown, theatrical pity in her voice. She looked back at me as she led the princess away. "Not if you have a consort who will strike a blow for love." She paused, and both women turned to face me. "Not if he can overcome his fine scruples long enough to set us free from the past."

They left me with the blank-faced lilies. I circled the garden until the flowers had closed and the grass was wet with dew. "To set *us* free," my mother had said. I remembered now the stone house where I'd found Cinderella, and the three women who had stood, open-mouthed, as I carried her off. My bride's step-mother, I realized with a dawning horror, might have been the very widow in whose easy embrace my father found solace so long ago. I thought of the simpering pair who had called Cinderella sister and kissed her farewell as we rode away. Perhaps those sorry women were more my sisters than hers! Had my mother waited, biding her time until she could work this hideous revenge? Had it been in her mind the night of the ball, when she'd leaned over the balcony and pointed out my love?

I did not go to supper that night but spent hours in my father's deserted chambers, reading his old decrees. There were edicts governing taxes and farming, commerce and war. There were gifts to churches and convents and bans on unfair tolls and tithing. In all these instruments, I found a voice I dimly recognized. Though many of these documents had been canceled by the queen's council, they spoke with kindness and respect to people who supported the crown through long days of endless toil.

This voice, this kindness, brought back a moment that until now had been lost to me. I saw myself and my father, on one of his rare stays at home, a brief sojourn between foreign wars. I was perhaps three or four years old and had played all day, without remonstrance, by his side. "You shall be a dandy prince, will you not, lad?" he asked, laughing as I put both my small feet into one of his boots. I laughed, too, hopping about in that giant buskin until I tumbled to the floor.

"You must not be a cruel king, eh?" He leaned down from above me, his smile suddenly vanished. "You must not rise by oppressing those below you." I remembered nodding then, because he looked so solemn, though I had no idea what he meant.

And now I searched through his legacy, the whole body of Royal Law. I saw no countenance of arbitrary execution there, no circumstance that allowed for punishment without a crime. When my taper at last failed and my eyes were closing on my own frightful visions, I stole softly to our bedroom and lay down beside my sleeping wife. I hoped I might dream, might travel back

to that day spent with my father, and ask him for advice. But I never slept at all, only lay awake listening to Cinderella's light and easy breaths.

The next day, neither my mother nor my wife left me any peace. The queen made speeches about loyalty and duty, while my love sat beside her, nodding like an eager puppet. Though I had hoped her natural kindness would dissuade her from such madness, she found every chance, even when we were alone, to plead for the death of her family. For three nights, she wept and relived the hurtful past, and nothing would move her from the queen's plan.

I did not realize how completely and with what horrible fidelity Cinderella was emulating her new mother until the fourth day after our conference in the garden. I woke that morning to find her still in bed beside me. At first, I was delighted to think she might have chosen my company over the queen's. As if to assure myself she was real and not a dream conjured up by my greedy heart, I touched a spun-glass curlet by her ear. "Good morning, friend," I whispered. "I am glad to find I married a stay-abed, after all."

But the eyes she turned on me were moist and ringed with blue shadows. Her skin was pallid, her voice small and tired. "It is not for pleasure I lie here," she said, "but rather for the lack of pleasure once I rise."

"Why? What is lacking for you, love?" I asked. "You need only tell me and it is yours."

She raised a pale hand to her forehead and looked at me through half-closed eyes. "I have already told you, and yet you will not save me from the demons that pursue me."

"What demons? Name them and they are gone."

"My stepmother and stepsisters," she said. "The ghosts who trail shame and pain, who walk abroad and flaunt my humble past. They are free to spread gossip while I am imprisoned by their evil tongues and cannot show my face beyond these walls."

"Nonsense!" I told her, cupping her chin in my hand. "Who would look on this countenance and believe it anything but noble and divine?" In truth, though, I was unnerved by her white lips and the feverish drops between her brows. "Why all this talk of blood and death from someone who lived for dreams only a few short weeks ago? Which of them has not come true?" I left the bed and pulled aside the drapes. The room grew brighter, but I felt strangely chilled. "What did you long for that has not come to pass?"

"You know well what it is I long for," Cinderella told me. She rolled onto her back and stared vacantly at the ceiling. "I want them dead. And if you loved me, you would want it, too."

The princess stayed in bed from then on. And because she claimed to be too ill for visitors, I was banished to my father's chambers. Each day when I knocked on her door, I heard muffled sounds, the scrambling of servants, and then was greeted by a maid, who told me Cinderella was in her bath . . . or with her ladies . . . or too weak for conversation. As spring turned to summer and summer to fall, I was admitted to her rooms only

seldom, and on each of these precious visits found her more wasted and wan than before.

So long as I refused to consider sending her family to their deaths, my wife lay exhausted in her bed. Her face, gaunt and anguished, reproached me, though she spoke few words now, only stared at me like a forlorn ghost. And if I sometimes caught sight of a brightly colored morning dress peeking from beneath her sheets, if I heard, occasionally, the vestiges of laughter and gay conversations cut short when I entered her domain, it mattered little. What pressed on me, what weighed on me night and day, was the absence of what I craved. The feeling that I had an ally who would stand with me against the cunning contrivances of court had dissolved. In vain, I waited for dreams of my father at night; in vain, I waited for my sweet friend to come to me by day. Until the waiting wore me down and I could stand it no more. The day I signed the order for the arrests, Cinderella began a steady, glowing recovery.

Which meant, of course, I saw even less of her than before. With her health, her appetite for royal amusements was restored, even doubled. There was no parlor game, no ballet or theatrical, no audience with pandering gossips, that did not find her sitting, dew-eyed and worshipful, beside my mother. Unless I chose to join in these empty pastimes, and I seldom did, I missed my wife more than ever. From my lonely waking to the evening meal, I was again deprived of the tender companion I had met at the ball. Only night drove her to our chambers, which she could

no longer deny me. But when we were alone at last, she would sigh deeply, as if to remind me that our time together was the price she paid for the glittering company of the queen.

The morning of the execution dawned chilly and fair. In the sewing room, where I went to find Cinderella, my mother pretended over her loom to have forgotten what day it was. She spoke of dresses and poets, but as her needle disappeared and reappeared above the cloth, I noticed an immodest shine in her eyes, an expectant, nervous gleam. "The princess," she answered my unspoken question, "has not joined us yet this morning. Perhaps she has need of some privacy today."

I hoped that it was true, hoped that, after all, my wife had found again the gentle heart I'd felt beating beside mine when we first danced. This ugly business must, at last, have sickened her soul. I paced the length of the room, feeling the same dizzying revulsion that had undoubtedly sent her into hiding. But where?

I decided to search the garden, thinking to find her weeping at the site where she had first begged me to put her family to death. I was determined, as I raced outdoors, to pull her from her knees, to forgive her pauper's greediness, to welcome home the bright and passionate child for whom I still pined. Perhaps, if we acted quickly, there was yet time to save her family's lives.

But the garden was empty, save for the blood-red roses and

the new buds that had sprouted to take the place of the blooms the queen had cut. As I started back to the palace, I met one of my mother's serving maids coming back from market. Wearing a rough brown cloak over her head and scrambling up the rock-studded path from town, the girl was in such a hurry, she nearly ran into me.

There was something in her furtive, headlong rush that made me certain of her mission. Though my mother feigned indifference, I knew she must be eager to confirm the executions. There seemed little doubt she had sent a servant to witness the gruesome spectacle. Suddenly, all my own guilt and anguish over the event seemed focused on this innocent messenger, and I stepped into the middle of the path to block her way. I could not bear to let her run to my mother with her bloody news; as if I could prevent the deed by barring its report, I grabbed the poor creature by the shoulders and ordered her to stop.

When the cloak fell away to reveal Cinderella's spun-glass hair, I backed away, astonished. "I saw it all," she told me, a broad, ingenuous grin lighting her face. "I even got a lock of Lucinda's hair!" Triumphant, she held up a curlicue of fine dark locks. I turned my head away as if it might burn my eyes.

"You should have seen the people!" she went on, her eyes shining. "They were all pushing and shoving behind me, but I stayed right up front. That is how I managed to get this lock. I walked up and pulled it off her before anyone could stop me."

I had not seen my bride so animated since the night of the

ball. She had forgotten all her lessons in refinement and was aglow with her old unbridled eagerness. "Their bodies did not twitch at all afterward, but you should have seen their eyes roll. I looked right at them, and I swear those three horrible heads knew just who I was!"

She was panting with excitement, as if she could not part with the details fast enough. "There really was not very much blood, you know. Stepmother bled the most, but that is because she fought the ax man hardest. You would not believe how she wriggled and cried out. Why, she was down on her knees before they even put her neck on the block. 'Fetch my stepdaughter,' she cried. 'Send for the princess! Tell her what they are doing to us!'"

Pausing for breath, she undid the cloak from her neck and stood, proud and radiant, in a pale yellow gown. "How I wanted to speak up and tell her I was there! I wanted her to look straight at me when the ax fell!"

My head was spinning, and a poisonous, bitter taste filled my mouth. I closed my eyes on her brightness, but her happy voice found me still. "Of course, a princess cannot afford to be seen in the streets like that. So I kept my peace and pulled this old cloak tight around me." She paused again, a touch of indignation softening her relish. "I only wish they had let me take a lock of Stepmother's hair, too. If the executioner had known who I was, he would never have dared push me away."

That night it was I who took to my bed. Pleading illness, I bid my wife good night at the door to our chamber and went to sleep again in my father's old rooms at the end of the hall. I was hardly guilty of deception, since the minute I lay down I was swept by trembling and nausea. I closed my eyes and, sweating mightily, let the waves of sickness wash over me. Their rhythm was some-how reassuring: the pain and then the brief reprieve, the quiet, hopeless space into which I could fit one or two breaths, suc-ceeded by the harsh, grinding pain. Absorbed in this pattern, sur-rendering to its awful symmetry, I fell at last into a dreamless sleep.

It was next day I met Lynette, a dairy maid in the palace stables. Of course, I had seen her before, plump and charming and care-less. She laughed too loud, slapped her thighs, and was forever picking straw from her hair. It was not hard to guess how it had gotten there. All the stable boys and several of the kitchen crew found endless excuses to tarry in the milking barn.

I could not blame them. As my own days grew emptier and my nights more hounded by guilt, I began to spend hours at a time lulled by her guileless chatter and her generous impulses. "If you like the milk of cows," Lynette took to telling me, wink-ing naughtily and cupping her mountainous breasts, "you shall find much sweeter here."

Day after day, I was drawn back to her like the rest. The queen and my princess never missed me, so there was nothing

to prevent my trips to the barn. Besides, there was something cleansing about the sweet breath of the cows and the steady rhythm of the buckets filling as Lynette milked. At first she took no special notice of my presence, but soon she must have sensed my need, my desperate case. She sent the others away and saved all her jokes and sly teasing for me.

In the beginning, these meetings were merely a way to fill idle hours, but now the scamp affords me pleasures as rich as any I fancied at that long-ago ball. My dairy maid is no princess, nor does she wish to be. But she lifts her skirts and wraps her dimpled thighs around me with a will. And I tarry longer and longer with her in the loft. As each afternoon fades into dusk, I rise reluctantly from our bed of hay. I push her from me, laughing. "Stop, Lady Lynette," I protest, bidding her cover herself and cease our play. "If I am any happier it must show upon my face. And for the sweet Lord's sake, help me brush this straw from my clothes."

Though in truth there is no need to hide, to proffer proof of my fidelity to Cinderella. She requires no troth, no lust, no love. She asks merely for the same tired recitation each night. As we lie in our silken bed, three times the size of the loft that I prefer, it is only the story she begs for, the same words over and over. And because it frees me in so many ways, I am not loath to tell the tale again. "The palace was bedecked with torches," I begin, "and young women from across the kingdom had come to the ball to meet their prince."

"And then?" she asks, her voice hoarse with longing.

"And then," I tell her, "a lovely stranger stepped out of a silver coach and into the prince's heart. She was more beautiful than any woman he had ever seen, more dazzling than a fairy queen."

Cinderella listens and nods, prompting me if I forget any part of the tired tale. She sighs and smiles, even as her eyes close and the story sends her off to sleep.

Evelyn's Song

*N*ow that witches are rarer than fish wings, most people don't know the first thing about magic. And the first thing about magic is that it hurts. When my aunt sent for the crone who lived at the edge of town, she meant only to scare me. So far as we villagers could tell, that foolish hag had never done more harm than give our night watchman a potion that made him mad for the weaver's widow. The object of his affections weighed at least twice as much as the poor man himself, yet their match was no stranger than many made without benefit of incantations or philters.

The marriage my aunt intended for me, I assure you, was far more ill advised and much more laughable. Yet she would have me wed Lord Brevington, a man forty years my elder. And she would have me curtsy sweetly before him, speak my little Latin, and play the harp. I, of course, would have none of it, and that is when the witch was sent for.

"You have humiliated me for the last time, my girl," Aunt Hazel scolded. "Nor will I permit you to demean the honest proposal of our dear guest." She nodded at this, toward Lord

Brevington, who seemed less demeaned than sleepy. He sat over the remains of Aunt's tea and scones, his head sinking lower and lower on his hollow chest.

But I sat with the harp beside me unplucked, reluctant to play the song she had bade me sing for His Lordship. It was "The Turtle Dove's Lament," a ballad that had found favor first with the court and then with all the unwed ladies in our town. The tale of a young woman abandoned by her love, it told of her standing above the sea on a towering cliff. She searched for her lost sweetheart's ship, clasped her pale hands across her breast, and leapt into the waves. The chorus, repeated three times, began with the words *"Your wild love has won me, now claim your prize."*

I could not, you see, sing that refrain to the grizzled gentleman on our settle. I dared not, for fear I would burst into laughter as I played. Indeed, one look at the poor old soul, his withered legs crossed under orange garters, had nearly undone me. "May I not play Your Lordship a sprightlier tune?" I asked. "'Derry Down, Derry Down,' say?"

My ardent suitor, who seemed to be snoozing, made no reply. So I begged my aunt instead. "Oh, please, Auntie Dearest, let me choose a song less passionate, more in keeping with the—er, age and state of our visitor."

I could not keep from smiling as I pointed at the napping noble, and my aunt was in a rage straightway. She scolded me so loudly, I was certain Lord Brevington would wake, but I need not have worried. It turned out that the good man had gone to a

deeper sleep than the two of us guessed, for when we tried to rouse him, we found that he was dead.

"Now see what you have done!" As if it were I who had caused the old man's soul to leave his body, Aunt Hazel grew an-grier still. "All our prospects, all our high hopes—dashed by a willful girl's stubbornness." She paced our small parlor like a trapped animal, sighing and calling on my dead mother to wit-ness her daughter's perfidy. At last, she summoned Lord Brevington's footman from the kitchen. And then she called the witch.

I was not afraid of Dame Meredith; I had grown up used to the sight of her bent form hobbling through the crowd at market, the sound of her nanny goat's bell when it wandered, as it often did, into our yard. So, after our noble visitor had been dispatched to his castle and Dame Meredith had arranged her musty skirts across the same settle from which Lord Brevington had taken leave of the world only moments before, I felt no alarm. Even when Aunt Hazel demanded an enchantment of the highest or-der, one that would ensure I learned my place, I never dreamt homespun magic could prove any more potent than the scolding I had just endured.

It required only a pinch of time, a trifling minute, to change my life. As soon as the dame had raised her arm and begun her chant, I felt the stiffness invade my limbs. *"Ye shall not rule the*

roost, ye shall not call the tune." As she recited the words, the old woman spread her knobby fingers like a cap across my head. *"But shall serve your master with nary a boon."*

It happened so quickly that even as I smiled at such nonsense, my legs went numb and I closed my eyes against a sharp pain that filled my chest. *"With a lively will, though it be not your own, ye shall do my bidding and make no moan."* No sooner had the pain stopped than my aunt screamed and I opened my eyes. I found that, indeed, my chest had been ripped open and that a shining bone erupted from between my breasts. I suppose it is a testament to the crone's witchery that I now felt no discomfort. I was dismayed only that my dress was ruined and my flesh turned the color of the coins my aunt had fished from Lord Brevington's doublet as he lay beyond the cares of earth.

Stranger, or should I say more horrible still, I saw that from the golden mote which pierced my chest, in a formation I knew only too well from hours and hours of practice, hung twenty harp strings. And where were these strings fastened? Why, all along my body, which, as I have said, had turned to burnished gold. I wanted to scream just as my aunt had when I saw, at the place where each string pierced my shining flesh, tiny blood drops lined like buttons up and down my chest and belly and thighs. But I could no more scream than speak or make the slightest movement to free myself from the spell that held me fast.

"What have you done, you foul fiend?" Aunt Hazel was crying now, beating the old woman about her venerable head. "Bring her back this instant, bring her back!" When her tormen-

tor stopped to wipe her eyes, the hag rushed for the front door, but Aunt yanked her by the apron strings and forced her to stand before me.

Dame Meredith, squirming like a pig in my aunt's grasp, seemed as surprised as anyone at her handiwork. "'Tis only a minding spell," she protested, staring at my strings, my golden limbs. "'Twill make dogs obey and keep horses from leaping the fence."

"My niece is no dog, beldame." Despite my peril, I was moved by Aunt's tears and would have comforted her if I could. "You have pierced her through and turned her still as stone."

"I meant no harm, mistress." Meredith reached out to touch me, then pulled her hand back as if she had felt fire. "No harm at all, I swear."

"Undo your spell, witch," Aunt Hazel commanded. "And be quick."

"I cannot." The fear in the dame's eyes made it all too clear she spoke the truth. "I do not know how." She explained to Aunt that no one had ever asked her to reverse the spell; everyone preferred dogs that minded and horses that stayed where they were put.

But Aunt Hazel would not rest till the witch had tried to unspell me. And tried. And tried. Finally, exhausted and hopeless, the old woman threw her apron over her head and wept as if her heart would break. "'Tis no use, my lady," she sobbed. "The child will not wake. She lives only to obey."

"Obey?" My aunt, nearly as tired as the witch, gathered the

strength to shake our neighbor by the shoulders. "What do you mean?" she asked.

"Whatever you last wanted her to do, madam," Meredith told her, "is what she will do forever."

"I wanted her to play." Aunt Hazel looked at me now, her voice as small as a child's. "I wanted her to play a song."

"Then you have only to ask it," the witch told her, drying her eyes and making for the door. "Perhaps it is not so bad, after all." She sniffled as she lifted the latch, ducked her head at me. "You need not feed her, from the looks of it, and 'tis certain that wayward child has learned to obey."

Aunt Hazel, I suppose, had neither the strength nor the will to chase after the old woman. For she sat where she was, long after the hag had left, staring vacantly at the fire and only sometimes at me. "It was just one song," she said at last. "Not so much to ask." She shook her head and tears collected in the ridges under her eyes. "Not so much to give."

That was when she stood and faced me, holding up one hand as the horse trainers do at Tinley Faire. "Play," she ordered, and lowered her hand again.

I tried to run from the feeling that rose in me as she uttered her command. I found, however, that I was frozen into a crouch, my folded legs held fast by the longer strings of the fiendish harp. So there was no escaping the rush of song that filled my chest and wanted to force itself from my throat. I had seen wrens and doves trembling in the throes of their songs, their tiny bodies

convulsed in the effort to set them free. And now here was I, equally in thrall to a melody I must release or die.

My mouth opened and the song poured out. My golden arms rose, without my willing it, to pluck the strings attached to my own breast. The pain and the joy I felt as the music echoed in my chest made me remember the smile on Our Crucified Savior in the church at Warwick's Ford. I marveled at the exquisite torture I was inflicting on myself, and would not have stopped it for all the world.

As I plucked and sang the very tune she had been unable to make me play a few hours before, my aunt stared at me in horror. Her mouth open, her eyes wide, she listened, as still as a statue, to "The Turtle Dove's Lament." When the last note had ceased shaking my poor bones, she woke as if from a trance.

"It is a beautiful tune," she said, staring into my unblinking eyes. "But I would rather die than hear it again!" Poor Aunt sank to her knees before me then, begging a forgiveness my frozen lips could never speak. "This is not what I intended," she cried, rending her dress and pulling her hair out in great fistfuls. "This is not what I meant at all!"

It was only a week before my aunt succumbed to the shock my transformation had caused her already tender constitution. Unable to help, I watched in horror as she grew ever weaker and finally, whimpering like a starving animal, let death put an end

to her suffering. Nor could I call out to those who buried her and sold all her possessions to the scrap dealer. Except for the harp, the great golden harp in the shape of a kneeling girl.

None of the greedy folk who bought me (each paid a handsome sum, and then recouped it by selling me for even more to someone else) could make me play the way my aunt had done. It was only a monster, a murderer and thief, who was able at last to put the magic to work. I suppose he was accustomed to giving orders, to treating others like dogs, for once he had stolen me from my owner and climbed the mountain to his palace, he did not sit beside me and try to pluck my strings as the others had. Instead, he pointed his terrible finger at me and thundered, "Play!"

That was the first concert I sang for the giant, but hardly the last. Just as all the tales say, he loved to listen to his magic harp. In fact, it became a ritual for him each evening after supper. No sooner had the dishes, with their mess of gnawed bones and rejected bits of gristle, been cleared from the table than the huge fellow would count the money he had made off with that day, call for his magic pullet to lay a golden egg, and at last demand of his wife, "Where is my golden harp?"

I often wondered if the little russet hen were under an enchantment, too. Perhaps she was a young girl like me, or even a good dame who had offended some magician or spell-weaver. Perhaps it cost her the same pain and gave her the same throbbing joy to lay her eggs as I experienced when I sang my songs? Often, when the giant lifted the bird from her nest and commanded, "Lay!" I felt the same loosening in my throat, the same

heat in my veins that accompanied my songs as they rushed, like air from a bellows, out of my chest.

The giant never went to church, and I doubt that he was acquainted with the Bible or with Our Sweet Lord. But I think he knew something of beauty and of holy sorrow. For when I sang for him, his dreadful face became composed, his eyes closed, and he acquired the devoted, worshipful expression of the parishioners back home. He never needed to tell me which songs to play, for as a result of my enchantment, I knew without words what melody he wanted to hear.

The giant loved most the plaints of waifs and wanderers. Perhaps because he was an outcast himself, feared and scorned by the folk he terrorized, he wept each time I sang of loneliness. "Ay, ay," he would say, nodding his frightful head. "That is the way of the world, is it not? The sorry way of our sorry world." Then, a tear as big as a pillow on his mighty cheek, he would close his eyes and soon be snoring.

You may be surprised when I tell you my life with the giant was not a bad one. It is true I could not move or speak, except to sing, and that at someone else's bidding. Yet though my songs were not my own, the way they sounded first in my chest and then in my master's heart made them almost like hymns. It was as if I had been born to bring this savage creature peace, to soothe that massive furrowed brow, and to put all to sleep in that perilous place, where our castle clung to the rocky cliffs above a patchwork of little towns.

In between songs, I suffered not at all, feeling neither hunger

nor thirst. Sometimes I watched the giant's wife mend her husband's endless leggings or listened to the pair chat over their supper. But most days I slept away the time, waking only to sing and then slip back into dreams of dancing and talking and running just as I had before my enchantment. Some wise men say our time on earth is but a dream; if so, my life had changed little. I woke from sleep to serenade my master, to settle his heart and his house, then slipped back into the past, where I could still speak my mind and my own two feet still took me where I wished to go.

I cannot say exactly when the boy first came to us, when he sneaked in to change the regular rhythm of our days. I know only that even after we discovered he had stolen some of the giant's gold, no one was much disturbed. The giant's wife blamed herself. The young man had looked so lean and meatless, she explained: no good for one of her husband's hearty stews, no good for much except fattening up. So she had fed him and hidden him, hoping to surprise the old man with a treat one day. But the boy had betrayed her kindness and run off before he could be cooked, run off with a bag of yellow coins.

"Do not trouble yourself, Wife," the giant told her. "The little gnat took nothing of value, nothing I cannot get back twofold from his village below."

And it was true. So long as the hen was untouched and I played for him each night, the giant was content and life went on as it had before the stealthy boy's visit. The great man would

stumble home each afternoon with more gold, more jewels and trinkets. His wife and he would place them in bags in a store-room, where they remained untouched. There was, after all, nothing for them to spend the coins on; the giant had long ago frightened away all the merchants and tradesmen in his domain. On rare evenings he would ask for a bag and run his fingers through the shining coins, but the pleasure he got from that was nothing beside the way his spirits lifted when the hen ruffled and squawked and lay, like a miracle, a perfect golden egg.

But when the boy stole the hen, everything changed. The giant's wife must have guessed how angry her mate would be, for at first she lied. She told him the hen had wandered away and must have fallen off the cliff beyond the castle walls. But her husband, whose large nose was more sensitive than ten smaller ones put together, knew the boy had returned. "I smell him," he bellowed. "I smell that pesky troublemaker. Where be he, wife?" He began to stomp around the rooms downstairs, the stones jumping in their places with his every footfall. He tore the tapestries from the walls, peered under the tables and benches, and opened the chests and drawers. "Be he live or dead, I'll grind his bones to make my bread."

It was then that his wife, fearing for her home, pointed a shaking finger at me. "Play!" she commanded, and though she had never craved a song from me before, it was clear she needed one now. I felt it pour from my throat just as my fingers rose to find its notes. *"There will never come her like again,"* the ballad began. *"She was doughty and clever and true to the end."*

It was a song of mourning for a dead lover, but the giant knew it was meant for his stout little hen. He stopped, sat in his great chair, and clasped his head in his hands. He wept as I had never heard him, openly, like a great, tree-size child.

When the boy came back for me, I must have been dreaming of dancing a jig or chasing the cat from the pantry. It was only after he'd hoisted me onto his shoulders and was carrying me out the door that I found my voice. In all the years since I'd been spelled, I had never been able to speak. But feeling him struggle under my weight, sliding to one side of his back and nearly tumbling from his clumsy grip, was shock enough to spill the words from my throat. "Help, Master!" I half crooned, half moaned. "Someone is stealing me away!"

You have heard what happened next; all the stories tell how the sad tragedy played itself out. How the giant woke from the slumber into which my tune had lulled him; how he thundered, "Stop, thief!" and then gave chase. How the boy tightened his grip on me and ran as fast and as far as his short legs would take him. How my master followed after, old as he was, taking one lumbering stride for every ten of the thief's. And how, as my master tired, the boy was able to gain a few precious paces and lower himself down a vine that clung to the crags where the giant's castle perched. How he reached the ground and chopped the stem of the plant in two, sending the giant, his huge hands reaching for a hold in the sunlit air, crashing to his death at the bottom of the cliffs.

When my master fell to earth, the whole world trembled.

The boy who held me was knocked off his feet as the ground shook, and since he grasped me fast, the two of us tumbled and rolled together until we came to a stop at last, pinned under one of the giant's boots. The bells in the town were ringing nones by the time the young man's family and some villagers were able to bring a timber and pry the boot's toe high enough to set us free.

The boy and his mother had themselves a fine manor, though nowhere as big as my former master's castle. It lay at the end of a long road that snaked its way through green farmland and the humble cottages of their servants, field workers, and stable boys. Thanks to the money they had stolen from the giant, there was always a pleasant fire burning in the hearth of the great house. Nor was there any end to sweetmeats and pies and other delicacies, since the magic hen continued to lay her precious eggs at the lad's command. Settled in a place of honor by the hearth, she was fed as much corn as she liked and frequently pecked at the boy's mother if the woman raised her voice to him. Clearly, the bird felt her lot had improved, and she seemed not to miss the hilltop castle we two had left behind. As for me, I was glad enough to see my old friend, though her bright, unblinking eye betrayed no memory of the years we had spent under the same roof. I began to doubt she'd been enchanted at all.

I slept much of the day, just as I had in the giant's home, but when I woke there was no one to play for. My new owner was so busy showing off his costly clothes in church and at market,

so eager to attend dances and to court every young maid in town, he seldom fancied music at home. Even if he had, he learned early that he might not have his way with me as easily as he did with the hen. The first time he'd brought me into the house and set me proudly before his mother, he had pointed his finger just as he had seen my master do. "Play!" he'd commanded me, but I could find no tune in him. "Play!" he repeated, anxious to show what a fine treasure he had stolen. But while the giant and his wife had nursed slow, shy songs in their hearts, this boy seemed to need no music at all. My head stayed bent over the strings, my golden arms rigid at my sides.

"Perhaps there is another trick to it, lad?" the boy's mother guessed. "Mayhap you missed some magic word that makes it sing?"

"No!" The boy pushed me from him so roughly that my strings shuddered and I felt a cruel tug in my chest. "I watched that great ogre careful as careful," he insisted. "'Play' is all he said, and point is all he did." Once more, he aimed his finger at me as if it were a musket. "Play!" he roared.

"Still, 'tis a lovely thing, my sweet," his mother said, studying me as I sat, silent, where her son had placed me. "Tune or no tune, 'tis made of gold, I'll warrant. Mind how it shines and all." I sensed a timid ditty, the beginnings of a song, as she looked at me. But as she dared not command me, I fell back to sleep.

So they stood me next to the hen, then, and were pleased to have visitors praise their new harp, the very size and shape of a lovely girl. "The filthy monster placed a spell on that instrument,"

the young man would tell them whenever they asked if I might be played. He would pluck one of my strings, then let it fall back, soundless. "It may never be played by the pure of heart." That was enough, of course, to keep strangers from trying to coax a song from me, and the boy always boasted most of the hen, whose eggs he could be sure of calling forth. "Now look ye here, for a true wonder," he would say, lifting a glistening egg from under the uncomplaining pullet.

Though it was a lie and the giant had cast no spell to keep me his, it was the same as if he had. The lad and his mother no longer tried to play me, and, having no songs of my own, I remained silent. I sorely missed the times when my master's loneliness had pulled tunes from my throat. Alas, no one but me mourned his death at all. Until the villagers at last succeeded in heaping dirt over his great fallen body and constructing thereby a massive fortification outside the town's gate, my poor giant lay looking with unblinking eyes at an endless procession of curiosity seekers who traveled to see the slain monster. And, of course, to heap praise on "Jack, the Giant Killer," as they soon christened the boy.

Jack loved to meet a crowd of such travelers by the mountainous corpse and tell over and over how he had bested his fearsome enemy. "Fee, Fi, Fo, Fum," he would howl, loud and gruff as the voice of Death in a Whitsunday pageant. "Those be the very words this hell-fiend screamed when he came after me." He would brandish an imaginary sword, swirling it in mad arcs around the giant's arm or leg. "But I was not afeared, you know.

It required only a bit of derring-do to smash this clumsy oaf to kingdom come."

By the end of his tale, which grew and changed with every telling, young Jack had always made himself out the bravest, most courageous young man in all the world, one who richly deserved the coins and treasure he had pilfered from my master. And each time he recounted his glorious adventures, he was wont to bring folk home to gawk and make much of his hen and his golden harp. "Lest ye believe me not," he would tell them all, "here be the magic proof."

When the body of my old master was at last moldering under a vast hillock of earth and thatch, it was clear that the cocky young man who had killed him now had more time than he knew what to fill it with. There were no more travelers to listen to his tales of glory, and the prettiest of the village girls—the one on whom he had set his heart—grew tired of listening to her suitor talk about himself. (As he wooed her by the hearth, the hen and I were privy to most of their conversations and to her final announcement that she had decided to wed the mayor's son.) Suddenly, then, Jack remembered me.

"I shall take this magic harp to be restrung," he announced to his mother, only two days after his ringleted sweetheart had abandoned him. "Perhaps it was damaged when the giant fell. If I can make it play again, we will have some gay parties and mend my heart soon enough."

"But what of the giant's curse?" his mother asked. "I thought

only the black of heart could play her strings." Her expression as she studied me was half sorrow, half yearning.

"That was just a tale I told, Mother," Jack said. "I wanted to keep her safe from prying hands."

"Ay," the woman said, still watching me doubtfully. But when she glanced again at her son, she was once more his doting mother. "Why, lad, 'tis a fine idea," she told him. "And then you might take up that flute your father left. He played it like an angel, he did."

Jack was already dragging me from my place at the fireside. "Perhaps, Mother," he told her, wrapping me in a dark cloth, shutting out the light. "But think of the seasons wasted while I must learn to put my fingers just so on the stops. This harp will play by itself."

"Or there's the viol," his mother offered. "Your uncle says 'tis the favorite instrument at court."

"Mayhap, good dame." The young man's voice sounded agreeable, but he tightened his grip on the bundle he'd made of me. "Yet that one will take even longer to master. Besides, they've nothing like my golden harp at court."

So saying, he juggled me to his back and trundled me down the street before his mother might think of another instrument for him to play. We wound around corner after corner, and though I could see nothing through my swaddling, the cries of vendors, the smells of fish and pies, and the stench of chamber pots poured into the gutter, brought memories of my girlhood in my aunt's village rushing back.

At one turning, where my owner stopped, I thought we had reached the studio of the musician who would fix my strings. But I was wrong, for Jack began to yell and curse at someone nearby. "Have you no better bed than the street, old pissant? Out of my way, I say."

Clearly the young man's anger had gotten the best of him, for I could feel that he was kicking whoever blocked our path. He kicked so fiercely and with such hatred, I fell from his back and lay on my side, the cloth that had covered me undone and my eyes staring into a deep puddle where rain had collected between cobblestones in the street. I hadn't far to search to find the object of my owner's scorn. An old man dressed in beggar's rags, with a face as red as fire, lay curled like a baby against the vicious kicks.

When Jack stopped to catch his breath, the old man lowered his arms and glanced toward me. His yellow eyes narrowed, and when he had assured himself he saw what he saw, that I was not an airy dream brought on by mead, a smile cut his face like a knife. He stared at me now and held my gaze even after my owner had resumed his savage attack.

"Move on, move on, you worthless carrion," Jack screamed. He stooped to retrieve the cloth in which he'd wrapped me and began to beat the man about the head with it. "Are you deaf, you old turd? Get up and let your betters by."

It was then, while the young man yelled and the old one stared, that I felt, as strongly as ever I had at the giant's castle, a song well up in me. Though he did not point and he did not speak, I heard the beggar's command as clearly as if he had been

my dead master, leaning against a brocade pillow and bellowing, "Play!"

So I did. Right there, in front of my astonished owner, I reached out to pluck my strings. Once again, at long last, the painful ecstasy took me, and the words ran like a waterfall up-hill, charging from my throat: *"I once had a love that was truer than true."*

The old man's knees dropped from his chest, and both he and Jack were still as stones while I played. *"'Twas long ago when the world was new."*

I could see the woman in the beggar's eyes, a dark gypsy with a hungry, heart-shaped mouth. *"Kiss me once and kiss me twice and beg me thrice to stay."*

The man's eyes closed now and he lay as quiet as a sleeping babe. *"And keep me in your prayers tonight though I be far away."*

When the song ended, Jack turned to me, triumphant. "You *can* play, after all. And here I was about to spend a pretty penny to put the music back in you, sly wench." He gave the nipple on one of my golden breasts a tweak, then stepped carelessly over the old man, who still lay unmoving in the street. "Wait till they hear your songs now! They shall be begging to dance to my tunes, all the beauties in town." He bound me up in the cloth again and headed back the way he had come. "And won't she be sorry, Miss Proud Heart who would have none of me? Won't Miss High and Mighty pine to be invited, too."

But, of course, it did not happen that way. For when we got back and Jack called his mother to come see, when he removed

my covering and commanded me to play, he still had not a single song in his heart, and I remained silent.

"I fear the musician does not know his work, my boy." Jack's mother had settled herself on a chair for my concert but seemed little perturbed by its postponement. "You must take the harp back straightway and make him do it right."

"But I tell you, this harp played." Jack was yelling now, though his mother had done nothing to deserve his harsh tone. "Just by the miller's courtyard, right in the street, a song for all to hear." Jack would not rest until I played again, and two times, three times, he pointed at me and shrieked, "Play, you harlot! Play!"

Two times, three times, I felt no song to play and my head remained bent and unmoving above my strings. Even after his mother had urged him to come to supper, to forget about music until the morning, he ranted and raved and ground his rude thumb in my eyes. "You *shall* play," he promised at last, kicking me so that I landed on my side and clattered against the hearthstone.

"Look what you have done to the poor thing," his mother said. She stooped to set me right, took a handkerchief from her sleeve, and knelt down beside me. Making small clucking sounds like the hen when it settled to roost, she spat upon the cloth and used it to polish my head and shoulders. It is a sad thing, indeed, to put a name to something precious you have lost. So it was for me when the woman stroked and petted me. I felt, of course, neither the warmth of her hand, nor even the weight of her fingers against my golden skin. Yet the memory of touch—of embraces and holding hands, of strolling arm in arm, or jostling up against

a market crowd—all this came back to me so that I was loath for her to stop. But stop she did at last, rising and standing back, arms folded, to check her work. She looked at me with the same self-satisfied smile my aunt had often bestowed on a gleaming goblet or platter, then followed her son to table.

That was not the last time Jack's mother picked me up and rubbed me to a shine. My surly owner saw fit soon enough to hurl me again to the floor in a fit of temper. One night when Jack and a companion came home from hunting, they sat by the hearth to eat a late supper and drink toasts to their own prowess with bow and arrow. After many boastful toasts and too much mead, Jack forgot that there was anything he could not do. And so he pointed his finger at me and commanded me to play.

I tried, you must believe, to find a song in that bleary-eyed lad. As I listened, two shadows, one tall and the other short, fell across his heart. The tall figure sang to the smaller one, but though I knew it would serve me to hear the words, I could not make them out. Like a fairy tune from a faraway wood, his song was lost and dim. I remained as quiet, then, as any other harp without a master to play it, and I dreaded what my silence might cost.

Instead of getting angry, though, Jack laughed and bade his friend try his hand, too, at making me play. But the other hunter, who had just toasted his own skill in felling a pregnant doe, had no more music in him than Jack, and so the two of them pro-

posed at last to make their own songs. They laughed and roared tuneless ditties at each other till I dared to hope they would fall into a drunken slumber and leave me in peace.

It was not to be. For when the uproar woke Jack's mother, she came into the great room in her shift, her hair undone, and begged them be quiet. Perhaps because she had just been torn from a dream and a piece of it was still in her head, I felt how much she yearned for the earlier, simpler times she and her son had shared. Her despair at her laggard boy and her own regrets brought my arms to my strings: *"If I had a cow, a large brown cow, a jug of milk I'd bring thee."*

Even in their cups, the two friends were stunned by my new-found voice. Jack's companion looked as if he thought black magic was afoot, and Jack himself rose from his seat, startled from his stupor.

"If I had seeds and a patch of earth, I'd grow a sweet pear tree." I felt a small, warm pride as a dappled day half dawned in the woman's heart. *"And all the lords for miles around would beg me for to try . . . One small bite of that sweet pear, one glance from your fair eye."*

But I had no chance to sing the rest of her song, for Jack came toward me, anger blushing his cheeks, so that even in the light of a single candle, his face looked like a Turk's. "You sing for a beggar, do you?" he snarled. He hauled me from the hearth and lurched for the door.

"And now you think to sing all by yourself, do you?" He opened wide the door, howling into the night air. "Go sing to the

moon about cows and seeds. We'll none of your country airs!"
With that, he shoved me outside, slamming the door so that I
heard no more of his bluster and lay cradled in the grass till his
mother tiptoed out to rescue and polish me, then set me again by
the hearth. Once in the night, I thought I heard the trace of a
song in someone's dream. It might have been the pale shadow
tune I'd felt earlier in Jack. It was not bold enough to rouse me,
though, and I slipped back into dreams of my own.

Perhaps my song had emboldened her, or mayhap she intended
to dispose her son more kindly toward me. In any case, it was
Jack's mother who finally carried me to the musician's house.
She hired a fellow to hoist me onto a wagon and then drove into
town herself. While she visited the baker and milliner, the
sweaty little man to whom she'd entrusted me worked for hours
restringing and tuning, yanking and tightening until I thought
my chest would burst. At last he was done, and she drove home
to set me proudly before Jack. "Now ye shall hear this harp play
proper at last," she promised, pleased with herself and the pleasure I was sure to bring the spoiled young man.

"Are ye certain that fellow's done the job?" Jack asked.

"As certain as certain," his mother assured him. "For I
stopped on the way home and commanded it to play."

Indeed, she had. And when she'd pointed and ordered music,
I had felt a whole flood of tunes dammed up in her heart. They

were fair to drowning us both, and I'd had a hard time choosing which one she wanted most.

"And?"

"And it played as lovely as you please."

"And sang?"

"Like an angel in the house of the Lord."

"Well, then." Jack's greedy smile made his face almost handsome. "We shall invite the neighbors and have that musicale at last." He bade his mother draw up a guest list, making certain she included the maidens he admired most. "I will go to the butcher myself," he offered, "and fetch back some venison and lamb."

The party was held three nights later, when it appeared that half the town had assembled to hear me play. Or rather, to hear Jack order me to play. Dressed like a peacock, in apricot and turquoise silks, my owner moved from dame to damsel, offering his hand and honeyed words. He looked and acted very differently, indeed, from the fellow who spent most of his days lying about the house, gaming or drinking with his friends. Inside, though, he was no different at all, and soon he was to prove it.

When all were supped and seated, he bellowed, nearly as loudly as the giant, "Where is my magic hen?"

A servant lay a brocaded pillow before him, then set the hen upon it. She was now as plump and proud as any fowl I have ever seen, and when Jack shouted, "Lay!" she raised her head and chuckled serenely before stepping away from a glistening golden egg.

As always, all the onlookers gasped and begged to touch the

marvelous orb. As it was passed from hand to hand, Jack kept his eye on this latest treasure. All the while, he smiled and stroked the careless, preening hen.

Too soon, however, he tired of this familiar triumph and called out as the giant always had. "Where is my golden harp?" he thundered, though all could see the servant had fetched me and was placing me upon a tassled rug at his side. When all was still, Jack made a great show of rolling up his sleeves. He pointed a ring-bedecked finger at me and stared imperiously from under his brows. "Play!" he commanded.

You have surely guessed what happened next, for the lad still had no song for me to play, no melody I could draw from his heart. After my silence came the usual curses, and the tantrums. Jack tried and tried but could not make me sing.

Finally, just as before, I was carried to the door. In front of all his gaudy guests, my master proclaimed that a harp which didn't play was not worth keeping. The door was thrown wide and the entire company drew back from the night. It seemed to me Jack struck a pose, holding me on his shoulders, like Atlas with the world. Time seemed to stop, several ladies tittered nervously, and someone gasped. At last, though, he mustered all his strength and hurled me with such venomous fury that the strings were torn from my chest and I lay, as if dying, under the eaves of his coachman's shed.

Spells are supposed to be broken with good deeds. Or with the answer to a riddle. Or with true love's first kiss. But that is not the way the enchantment that bound me was at last undone. I doubt the bandy-legged giant-killer who hurled me from his house cared where I landed—but had he used only a little less arm or a bit more gentleness, the magic might not have been throttled out of me. And had his good mother rushed to retrieve me instead of giggling nervously and calling for more savories, I might not have fallen into that healing sleep.

When it was over, it was as if a dream had ended or a fever broken. I woke to the whickers and warm breath of a handsome bay, leaning from his stall to nibble my hair. I felt a tingling in my arms and legs, a ringing in my ears and skull, and the heady, dimly remembered rush of blood through my veins. Without knowing what I did, I raised myself onto one elbow and opened my eyes to the sight of my own two legs, my long-lost knees and shins. There was pain, yes. But nothing I could not endure, would not have suffered doubly, for the sake of what came next. I stood, sweet heaven, I rose up and walked.

Surely nobody noticed the poor girl who struggled to her feet by the stables. Who stood for a moment, eye to eye with the bay, then turned toward the open fields behind the great house. There were no words, only a rhythm in my head that moved my feet, that called my name, that drew me to the forest where the moon was setting.

When I passed the door through which I had been tossed—

was it moments or days before?—I heard no voices and all was still and dark. Yet as I left behind that sullen house, there came again the shadow song I had felt in someone's dream—was it days or years before? The two figures in the dream were clearer now, and I could hear Jack's father laughing, see him hoist his small son to his shoulders. He sang a tune to the little boy, a tune I could have played, music I might have sung. For the time it takes a candle to smoke and then go out, I lingered to listen. The pull to soothe my master, to find at last the song that would bring him rest, held me. But then I heard again the pounding in my ears, the rush of my own blood.

My song. Though I had been so long bewitched that I barely remembered what it was to have a will of my own, I heard a new tune now. No one had pointed at me. No one had shouted, "Play!" Yet clear as a stone dropped in a still pond, loud as the call of geese across the sky, I heard the music of my own heart. It played a stream burbling in the shade of apple trees, and the warm, solid thrum of waking bees. I had no words for my song yet, but the scent of fruited boughs and the rush of wind against my chest were as real to me as my own two feet.

Those feet, no longer made of gold, climbed the pasture gate and set out for the woods beyond. I raced forward, trampling damp grass until I came to the top of a rise. I stopped for a moment to look back at the great house below. Inside its sleeping windows were old songs, music that was dead to me, other people's dreams. I tossed my head, like a mare slipping its bridle, and flew into the morning, running as if I would never stop.

Diamonda

When I first saw her, the name caught like a prayer bead in my throat: Diamonda. I have never called her that out loud, of course. While she was in hiding with us, she used a simple maidservant's name, and now the troubadours have christened her Snow White. But those gossips were not there when we found her, arms and wrists smeared with blood, lips the color of crushed violets. She was not white as snow then, but I have spent my whole life prying gems from a mountain's belly. I don't need to see their faces cut and polished to know how they will shine.

Her tap on our door might have been the wind, or a branch in its fall, so soft was the sound she made. When at length I opened the door that night, she fell across the threshold, one arm landing so that her fingers nearly reached the fire in the hearth. Clotted with mud and covered with blood, she might have been old or young, man or maid. But then I found a cloth, stooped to wipe the dirt from her eyes, and saw what she was.

As I freed her face from the filth that hid it, my brothers' sighs were like the moans of souls raised suddenly from damnation to paradise. For the seven of us, grown to manhood without the

scent or touch of a woman, she seemed a goddess, some glory-streaming sprite who'd taken a wrong turn and stumbled into the real world, where goddesses could cut themselves on thorns, wander lost for days, take sick and shake with chills. How I wanted to rush outside and tear the dead roses up by their roots. How I yearned to bathe her in the pond at Fairny, to hold her until the water caught her fever and she lay sleeping in my arms.

Instead, I made a pallet beside the hearth and we stretched her along it as best we could. She lay, her head against our bundled cloaks, and stared at the ring of twisted faces, tiny bodies above her. Sometimes I wake in the night, as if an old wound is itching, and see again the horror that widened her eyes.

It was only seconds before her breeding asserted itself and the look of revulsion faded. "I am afraid I have lost my way." She wrapped the vestige of a skirt around her poor bruised legs. "I must ask your pardon and your charity." We all drew closer, our forgiveness palpable. She glanced at Corwyn and then at me.

"I am Erin," I told her. I stood posturing grandly while Dynll, more sensible in his adoration, grabbed the cloth from me, dipping it in the bucket of water we kept by the fire. "These are my brothers, and though we have dwarf bodies, our minds are as sharp, our hearts as stout, as any man's." Dynll pressed the cloth to her head, and I added a deep flourish.

But as I bent to her, I was consumed with a sudden, shameful jealousy and wanted nothing more than to wrest the cloth back from my brother's hand. I stood there twisting my belt like a simpleton, lusting to feel her hair against my hand, to wipe

sweat from the glistening hollow above her lips. "My lady," I managed at last, "we are at your service for as long as you wish."

"You are kind," she said. "And I am blessed to have found such gentle hosts in this accursed wood." Her cheeks flushed and her dark fawn's eyes rested on me. Had she known then how many years she would stay with us, how long she would shine in the midst of our deformity, she might have chosen to brave the snow and forest again, instead.

Her fever lasted three days. On the last morning, I was fixing a loose ax handle for Ferin and so let him take her the broth. (I'd risen before dawn to spend two hours nursing potatoes and a few old carrots into what I hoped would pass for soup. When Rowan had fallen ill that autumn, I could not remember where we had stored the tormentil. But now, like a falcon with God's eye, I found the last of the herb under a hearthstone and boiled it all with the stock.) So it was Ferin she thanked for the thin soup and, though he insisted he did not deserve it, I believe to this day she credits him with her recovery.

When we came back from the mine that night, Diamonda's fever had broken and she met us at the door. If she had seemed a broken flower beside our hearth, she towered above us now, no longer a touchable goddess, but bright and inaccessible as truth.

"Bless you all," she said, her hair freshly combed and braided down her back. She turned to Ferin with a smile that twisted the innards of every man in the room and struck poor Ferin

dumb. As she talked, he could no longer look the sun in its face and instead stared trancelike at his boots. "The soup you brought me this morning has worked wonders, Little Physician. For, as you can see, I'm quite recovered." She lifted the hem of her skirt as if it were a ball gown and spun around the room.

Her dance and the slice of thigh it revealed left us dizzy; no one could think of a response more clever than to moan and sigh as if we ourselves had fallen sick. "I wanted to fix you a feast to repay your kindness, but I am afraid all I could find was potatoes and cornmeal."

She chattered happily as she led us to the table. She had only covered it with a cloth, but somehow it looked different—more precise, more to be reckoned with than it had ever seemed before. There were eight places set, and she escorted each of us to a seat as if we were noblemen attending a banquet. "Here's your place, Good Doctor Ferin. And this chair's for you, Rowan. Now, Sir Dynll, if you will be so kind. And Corwyn. And Gwiffert. Here, Lord Timias. And you here, Fair Erin."

Dynll was the first to come to his senses. "How," he asked, "did you remember all our names?" His forehead, broad and corded with veins, wrinkled like a beggar's belly. His eyes misted with admiration.

She laughed. "How do you think I could ever forget them? Night and day while I was sick, I said them over like a cate-chism."

I sank into the chair she had pulled back for me. "Fair Erin," she had called me. I was torn between hope and humiliation.

Was she singling me out for a joke? I looked at my brothers, their swollen heads bobbing and gleaming in the lamplight. Was I, last born of seven freaks, the most freakish? Of the distorted carnival masks turned like dark flowers toward her brightness, was mine the most hideous of all?

Warily, I studied my Diamonda as she filled each plate with the pebbly pancakes she had coaxed from our potatoes and meal. Her eyes shone with pride and good intentions; there was no hint of the disgust that had flashed across them when we met. And her lips? They were parted in a smile, full as a child's and as impossible not to return. They exonerated her completely.

She had spoken without malice. But did that mean, I wondered late into the night while the others slept, that I was actually not hard for her to look at? I had seen the children at Genfall Fair whisper and draw back, tiny rosebuds closing all along my way. I myself had stirred my reflection in a stream, frothing the water until the shards of face under my hand could have been anyone's, even a normal man's. I knew better than to hope that she found me handsome or fine-featured. But still, alone with the sort of timid dream that springs to life only near sleep, I thought perhaps Diamonda might have found me a well-turned dwarf!

It was weeks before she trusted us with her secret, weeks that seem now the gentlest of preludes, idle days free from whispers and bolted doors. It was then that I took Diamonda ice fishing in the pond that lies past Fairny Caves. While the wind of envy

rattled and moaned, closing its fingers around her hiding place, the two of us spent whole mornings in the blue shadow of the mountain beyond our forest. Careening down ice-covered bluffs on a makeshift sled, we traveled toward the dearest friendship I have ever known.

I remember how she would kiss me for luck, her lips burning my cheek before our descents. How she would throw back the cape from her face and laugh when one of our croppers landed us, splay-legged rag dolls, in the snow. How afterward, she would sip my chamomile tea, weaving our damp adventures into stories for my brothers. And how she would stay up with me long into the night, talking about such foolish, inconsequential things that I will never love anyone so much.

Not that she wasn't fond of us all. Not that she didn't take pains to memorize each of our likes and dislikes, our moods, just as she had our names. But—and I know my dwarfish dreams do not deceive me here—there was a special look, a way of smiling, a tone of voice, she saved for me. The others noticed it, too. Sometimes they teased, but more often they acknowledged the distinction, the primacy that Diamonda's silent preference bestowed. "What should I shoot for dinner?" Rowan would ask me, the huge quiver slung over his shoulder. "Does she like squirrel?" Or, after we had eaten and she was turning the spindle by the fire, Corywn would steal to my side. "How can I tell her without hurting her pride?" he'd whisper, his hands hidden in the dangling, overoptimistic sleeves of a jacket she had made for him. "You know how to put things to her."

It became a nightly ritual, the others climbing to the loft for bed while Diamonda and I stayed by the hearth to talk. And so, if she had something hard to tell, it was only natural that I was the one she chose to share it with first. But I would rather any of my brothers had taken my place that night, had sat beside her sipping tea, and heard her speak of leaving.

"I didn't tell you before," she said, watching the orange village at the bottom of the fire tumble into ruin, "because I couldn't bear to worry you." The light from the fire caught a swelling, a shine at the edges of her eyes. "But surely you see now that I endanger you all by staying. We must say goodbye, dear friend."

I was the first, then, to hear how the queen had driven away her lovely stepchild. Long before wetnurses whispered it to children at bedtime and courtiers banished it, with a wave of their ringed fingers, to the exile of stale gossip, the fairest woman I have ever seen told me her story. It did not surprise me at all to learn that Diamonda was of royal blood—for me, she shone as brightly in our thatched cottage as she does in the palace that is now her home. What *did* astound me, though, was the idea that anyone anywhere could wish her harm.

"How could your mother put a price on your head?" I asked. "How could flesh turn against flesh?"

"She is not my mother, Erin. My father used to tell me he dreamed my mother." The firelight found her frown, kissed it with honey. "When I was little, it made Father sad to speak of her. Each time I asked what she looked like, he would only lean on my arm and make me take him to the huge mirror in my

stepmother's bedchamber. He would stand me in front of it and stare over my head into the glass. 'There,' he would say, 'That is what your mother looked like.'"

I cannot remember my own mother, but I know she was not a dwarf. I know because of the wine pitcher that Timias bought at Genfall. As Diamonda spoke, I glanced up to where it rested above the hearth. The comely woman holding grapevines on the handle might have been our mother's twin; all my brothers said so. When I was a child, something stubborn, some unschooled weed of pride, sprouted in me each time they told the story of my birth. Too weak to lift her head or open her eyes, my mother had smiled at them as she held me tight. "This one," she'd said, "is fine as a prince. He's a dear, normal little lad, isn't he, boys? I told your father it would be different this time. I wish he could see what a strapping son I have borne!"

"Ah, yes," my brothers told their dying mother. "Here's a healthy, normal babe for you at last." They had crowded around me, patting my ugly head, kissing my withered limbs.

"Just look at his handsome face," crowed Rowan. "And his body," admired Gwiffert, "how firm and straight it is!" "He will be as tall as an oak," promised Timias, tears blinding his eyes. "As strong as any man for miles," wept Dynll.

Only Ferin and Corwyn, too young to play the game, began to protest that the baby's head was much too large for its body, that its eyes bulged horribly from their sockets. So they were banished from the room and did not see our mother sigh, draw me to her, and whisper in my ear, "The best for last, sweet Erin.

I saved the best for last." Dynll says I never cried until they took me from her arms.

The fire was a gray powder, but still I could not let Diamonda go. "There is no reason to run away," I insisted. "This poor place is probably the last spot on earth your stepmother's soldiers would look for you. Why, you could stay safe here forever while that greedy monster tears up the country for miles around."

"I wish it were true, but the smith's wife told me today there's a brigade of royal troops camped near Higman's Crossing." Diamonda poured the last of her tea over the ashes, then bent her head over the empty cup. "I wonder why the money isn't enough, Erin. She has all of Father's fortune. Why does she need my death?"

"Perhaps," I said, stiffening with pleasure as she took the hand I offered, "your stepmother is afraid you will change your mind about renouncing your inheritance. She has only to look at you to know there is no man alive who would not fight to the death to support you."

The more she smiled, the more I wanted to prove my words, to show her I meant what I said. "To the death, I swear it!" I yelled, struggling to my feet, Punch determined to fell giants.

"Many thanks, sweet Erin." She was whispering now; my battle cry already had the others stirring in their sleep overhead. "But your death would hardly please me." She stood then, too, and put her hand on my shoulder, which shook like a thing

apart. "What you *can* do for my sake is sleep well tonight and help me tell the others in the morning."

Sleeping well was an art I lost that night. When they learned how close the troops were, my brothers decided to spread the story in the village that our visitor had gone back to her home and family. This precaution, though it proved necessary, forced Diamonda to live like a prisoner in our dark cottage. And I? I lay awake each night, grieving her loss. Who is warmed by a transient sun? What sort of reprieve was it to live with the knowledge she would have to leave us?

As the days wore on, Diamonda was no happier than I. Each morning, as we left for the mines, our royal stowaway seemed more nervous, less patient. She seldom complained, but her eyes were distant and uncertain, her songs turned sad, and she paced when she walked. "I feel as if I am on a draughts board with nowhere to go," she told me one morning. "At least let us steal out after sunset, Erin. We can skate by moonlight and you can tell me all the stars' names, the way you used to." She made it sound as though she were yearning for something that had happened years ago instead of weeks. And she made it impossible for me to say no.

We waited until well after dark, then set out with torches across the snow. When we reached the pond, she ran toward it with a little shriek of delight. She stooped to put on the skates I had carved her from a yew branch, then, like a finch loosed from its

cage, sped out onto the ice. "Hurry up, Erin!" Her shadow darted and wove over the shining ground. "Look—I have already learned to skate backwards!"

Though I would have been content to stand and watch her forever, I put on my skates and followed her onto the sheet of moonlight. I have been skating as long as I can remember, and though she learned quickly, I still had a few tricks to teach her. She liked my leaps the best; she held her breath before each jump and clapped like the villagers at a juggling show when I came down. I was skating to the farthest edge of the ice (having de-cided to leap across a log stranded in the middle of the pond) when I saw the lights.

They were a good distance away, that I could tell. But how fast they were advancing was harder to judge. I raced back to where she stood and grabbed her hand. I pointed to the torches, twinkling like stars on the slopes above the stream. "If they are on horseback, we have no time to get home," I decided, already skating away from the cottage. "We will hide in the mine."

We took off our skates and stumbled through the snow, cut-ting west toward the far side of the hills down which the lights were filing. "It lies just ahead," I told her, battering my way through drifts that reached my hips. She followed gamely, less en-cumbered by snow that came only to her knees. But fear had taken her breath, and she sucked in the icy air too deeply as she ran.

When we had reached the entrance to the shaft and worked our way down to a point where our torches were hidden from view, I stopped and made her rest. I climbed back to the surface

to drag a branch across our tracks and seal the entrance behind us. "We are safe enough now," I told her when I returned, "unless your stepmother's men can see through stone."

She would not sit but remained pinned to the wall of the shaft, gulping air as if it were water, her body shaking, her eyes closed. When the pounding of hooves echoed in the cave, she ran to me and threw her arms around my neck. Her chest was heaving and I could feel her heart jump against me. As the men aboveground yelled to one another, I put my arms around her, too, and forced her to sit on the ground, soothing her as I would a child. "Shhh. Do not fret. I will not let them harm you."

I knew our mine as well as I did my own house. I was calm and certain of our hiding place. "There is no need to worry," I whispered, my breath spreading smoky fingers in the gloom. Still she shuddered and held me close, breeding in me a kind of madness, a sharp desire to prolong her anguish. For as long as the men remained dismounted and their footsteps crossed and recrossed the ground above our heads, Diamonda melted into me. As long as they continued to yell and laugh, her sweet breasts were mine to press against, to feel with arms that fell slyly, secretly against her time and time again.

We remained undiscovered, and when the horses had clamored off over the hills, we were free to go home. But not free to risk again such foolish expeditions. Even Diamonda now saw the sense in her confinement and begged no more for moonlight skates. Our caution doubled and our lives rattled like dried pods. My brothers and I became prisoners, too, circling dully between the mine

and the cottage, afraid to take trips to town, deal with traders, or let beggars in for food. In the center of our weary pattern, Diamonda grew more and more restless, her only entertainment the quiet talks she and I shared after the rest had gone to bed.

"Do you suppose," she asked me one evening halfway to spring, "that you and I want what is best for us?" She was mending a tear in the vest I had bought from a peddler. I had noticed often how the slow, regular passage of her needle through cloth turned her philosophical. Now something crumbled and gave way inside my chest as she pricked herself, sucked her finger, and sighed. "Do you suppose God has arranged it so that human desires are like seedlings bending toward the light?"

My body was a stream swollen with a sudden thaw, racing toward things it could not see. "What do you mean?" I asked.

"Oh, I know it sounds wicked," she said, eyes once more lowered to her sewing. "I used to have a tutor; he was a priest. He told me that the body desires but the spirit is always satisfied. Do you think that is so, Erin?"

The sound of rushing water filled my ears. I looked at her, helpless with longing. It was a longing of the flesh, yes. But of the mind, too. And of the spirit, surely, since I would gladly have accepted transformation into the mindless, sexless cloth she worked, just to be nearer her. "What do you crave, dear friend?" I asked her, trembling at the thought that it might be something I could give.

She looked up from her mending, her whole face flushed the way it had been when she was ill. "You will laugh at me."

"I could never laugh at you," I protested. "Or deny you anything you ask for. Only tell me what you want." *Before I explode with need,* I should have added, with the frustration of heaven glimpsed through a keyhole, a distant horizon that calls and calls.

"Perhaps it is wrong to want more than we already have," she said at last, no longer looking at me, staring instead at the smoking hearth. "But my dream is so stubborn, so dear, I cannot give it up. I think I know what love is, Erin, though I have never tasted it." Still she could not bring herself to look at me. The cause, to my mounting joy, was not my appearance or any aversion she had to it. The flush on her cheeks, her downcast eyes, suggested instead that her native modesty struggled against a consuming passion. "How strange, how sad that I am most awake when I sleep, when he whose touch I have never known opens me like a flower."

One of my brothers turned in his sleep above us. The wind outside howled and beat itself against the door. The moon stopped rising and waited, caught in the window. "Who?" I asked. "Who is he?"

"Someone I know," she told me, staring still at the ashes, "as well as I know myself. Someone who has helped me bear sickness and poverty. Someone whose face I carry like a dear, familiar secret wherever I go."

What had been a pale shoot of possibility was now a monstrous delight that out-howled the wind and filled me with a vanity and courage I had thought reserved for larger men. "I never guessed," I said, standing and walking to her, "that you were yearning for what is near to hand!"

I bent to her now, a good child rewarded suddenly with his fondest wish, a pious zealot about to collect the answer to his prayers.

"You are right," Diamonda told me. "He is no further than my dreams." She, too, had gained courage and was finally looking me full in the face. "His kindness, his devotion, are as close as my heart. His handsome smile, his tall and graceful form— they wait only for me to close my eyes."

Poor deluded dwarf! Now the current that had buoyed me up closed over my head. A drowning man, I sank down beside her chair, my face in my hands. "'Handsome'?" I repeated. "'Tall'?"

"I knew you would laugh at me." She shook her head, stroking the velvet vest in her lap. "In truth, Erin, I do not blame you. Here I am, a penniless princess dreaming of a man I have never even met!"

Again she shook her head. "Sometimes I think I will manage it, my friend. I think I can be content to stay here with you and your good brothers. And then I go to bed and he is with me again, wooing me away, calling me past any delight I have known."

That night, though I mouthed platitudes and urged Diamonda not to abandon hope, I buried mine. Just before dawn snuffed out the moon, I smashed the wine jar with the beautiful woman on its handle. I threw it with all my might against the hearth and watched it shatter against the stones.

Perhaps Diamonda, too, lost heart. Perhaps she began to fear she would live forever with her diminutive admirers, and never meet her handsome dream. Perhaps that prospect was worse

than returning to the trap she had sprung. Why else would she have let in the old beggar woman? Why believe in winter apples, when all around her was ice and chill? Unless, somewhere, in the secret reaches of her dreaming heart, she had chosen to die?

The others found her first. I had taken to waiting behind, watching to make sure no one followed us home. When I walked in, my brothers were standing in a hushed ring around her. She lay as if, overcome by weariness, she had decided to take a nap on the floor. Her cheeks were still flushed, her skin warm. The apple had rolled from her hand and stopped, wine-colored and immense, just short of the ashes in the hearth. Though it looked fresh picked, plump with sun, a horrible stench filled the room. Had she noticed the smell when her first bite broke the skin? Had she welcomed the poison, inhaled it like perfume as she fell?

The foul odor and the purplish skin of the fruit made me certain it had been tainted with belladonna. Of the seven of us, I had learned the most about healing and herbs. But Diamonda was beyond my help. If she had been felled by henbane or hemlock, I would have set to boiling nettles in hopes of reviving her. If her heart had been stopped with mistletoe, I would have asked Dynll to climb Corwyn's broad shoulders and reach me the mandrake roots we had hung to dry from the rafters that fall. But I knew no remedy for the poison that had by now spread its silent tyranny to every part of her.

I placed my thumb on her wrist and my ear to her breast—

how many times in the years ahead was I to find my head against that precious pillow, hearing nothing but my own racing heart! My brothers closed around us, expectant, hushed. I told them she was neither dead nor alive, but gripped by a poison that had stolen her faculties and sealed her body like a tomb.

We put her to bed as we had when she first came to us, stretching her across a pallet by the hearth. It was not until she was covered with all the blankets we could find, until she slept like a frozen bird beside the grate, that I heard the strange roar start up among us. When the rest drew back silently and left me standing alone beside her, I realized it was me I'd heard, wailing like a wolf and beating my fists against the hob.

It was Ferin, always best with his hands, who built the crystal cocoon in which we placed her. "What if there is a change?" he had asked. "What if she wakes and needs us? Erin says she isn't dead, and I will not bury her alive." So we felled a maple, and he carved a bed for her. While he fashioned wooden angels and rosebuds, the rest of us contented ourselves with bringing home what gems we could and setting them in a necklace for her to wear. When the bed was done and we had laid her in it, Ferin covered her with a casket all paned in glass so we would be sure to notice if she stirred.

Fearful lest the queen discover our sleeping treasure, we hid her bier in a small shed behind the cottage. There, each of us in turn stood guard beside her, waiting for miracles. But Diamonda

never moved. As winter withdrew slowly like a beaten cat, and green buds pushed through the forest floor, she dreamt on, unchanged. When the woods around her sounded with restless mating calls, she lay as beautiful and perfect as a stone saint in church. When spring had spent its promise and summer, too, we kept a fire going and wrapped our hands in wool while Diamonda felt no chill. At last, when ice stretched once more the length of Fairny Pond, only the seven of us were a year older than when we had laid her in her bier.

I kept the juice of the apple in a stoppered vial. I mixed herbs, concocted tinctures to find an antidote for the poison it contained. As the years passed, scores of squirrels and rabbits met their death at my well-intentioned hands. First I would poison the little beasts and then work my latest cure. All to no avail. It gave me hope, though, this foolish doctoring; it convinced me that I worked for her recovery. For as long as I kept meddling with my potions and powders, I told myself, I was surely as anxious as the others for Diamonda's deliverance.

Though, in truth, I had less reason to be. Because so long as she lay still and lifeless, I could be with her the way a man—a real man—was meant to be with a woman. Or very nearly. As nearly as a repulsive dwarf dared. If it has been torture to remember this, then it is damnation to tell.

For whenever it was my time to stand guard at her bed, I lay beside her instead. How could I see her, desirable beyond endurance, and not lift the cover that separated us? How could I

stoop to kiss her cheek and not beg her forgiveness by burying
my face in her breast?

It was always the same. I began by swearing I would not come
near her. I stood at one end of the hut while she lay, streaming
radiance, at the other. I told myself I could do as the others did,
could serve my love without demeaning her. And so I clung to my
side of the tiny room, wrestling demons that would have given a
giant a stout match. When I turned, it was only because I
thought perhaps she had wakened and might need me. All innocent concern, I would make my way to her side and lean over just
to make certain she had not called faintly from beneath the glass.

She had not called, of course, but lay as always, a candied
sweet. The jewels we had scavenged from our poor mine seemed
cloudy against her lustrous throat. Day after day, the hope was
fresh each time I looked inside the glass, each time I watched for
the damp print of breath on its face. And so, telling myself I
might have missed her cry, her muffled call, I swung open the
casket and bent to feel her pulse.

Once so close, I kindled like an oil-fed blaze. Ferin had made
her bed long and broad, broad enough for two. Tingling with
shame and a rough, unstoppable need, I climbed in beside her.
Too late then to curb the hunger that guided my fingers. Too late
to reprimand the wicked, insatiable dwarf who stroked and
kissed and licked. Her hands, her face, her perfect breasts that
waited just beneath the corded neckline of her loosened gown.

Is there a reward for taking the devil's hand but refusing to

dance? Is there a place in hell, less loathsome than the rest, for those too small of soul to finish the evil they begin? If so, I am spared the ultimate punishment that would be mine if I had once been able to take Diamonda in her bier the way I did each night in my restless, guilt-stained sleep.

Because I did not. Always, when I reached lower and, with a thousand tears and apologies, began to lift her skirts, I saw not my own dream but hers. As I touched her, shaking with fervor, I watched my hand become large and fine. The fingers lengthened and straightened into those of someone else, the palms grew line-less and white. And as I tried to lower myself onto her, I felt my body change. My legs were charged with power, thick and long and coiled with strength; my arms lost their withered crook and looked as smooth and graceful as an acrobat's.

And my face? I cannot tell you how I saw it, but I did. And I felt the transformation as clearly as you feel an icy spring rush against your skin. My bloated head grew slender, handsome, my eyes and nose as perfect as Diamonda's. I was, for a moment, what I had always yearned to be—Diamonda's dream. Locked in-side this new and chiseled form, I watched my sweet love reach out to me. She stirred in her sleep and put her arms around me. But as she drew me to her, blind and doting, the horrible dwarf twisted free and ran from the hut to stand sobbing with his back against the wall until his watch had ended.

Year after year, her dream vanquished me. Night after night, I lay in my bed, rubbing and rocking, while Diamonda, chaste still, waited for her prince. If I had been the one on watch when

he came, I would have known him, disguised or not. As it was, he wore a deep-hooded cloak and told Gwiffert he was a healer from Wainport across the mountain. By the time my brother had raced to the house to fetch us, the stranger had the casket open and was holding her in his arms.

He had thrown the cloak back from his face, and his light, curly hair was like a flame above the dark tangle of hers. His features were as I had always seen them—bright, comely, and ripe with enchantment. She was already awake and looked, for one dazed moment, away from her redeemer toward the seven manikins clustered at her waist.

As she turned, so did he, and twin suns beamed down on us. Her lips parted but she did not speak, as if she had forgotten during her long sleep how to form words. Then, after roving over us all, her eyes seemed to fix on me. A nameless shadow darkened her smile, and the shame of my old longing swept me.

"How long have I been sleeping?" Now her eyes found his again, though we could have answered her better.

"They say for years, my lady," he told her, his gaze locked on her face as if it were the north star. "Though, to tell the truth, I think I have slept all my life until now."

She laughed. It was not the same delicate, embarrassed laugh I remembered, but long and sparkling and laced with delight. "It seemed like no time," she told him. "I dreamed of you and did not want to wake."

Now she lives with him. Sleeps beside him and wakes when he does, her legs tangled with his, her hair caught under the pillow they share. When he holds tribunal, he keeps her next to him and will not render judgments until she and he agree. Sometimes, when she questions his decision, they argue and draw apart, strange, hooded looks clouding them. But it is nothing, a storm in a summer garden, the confusion of leaves before they fall and lie together, limp and spent. Diamonda dreamed him before they met, brought him with her out of her dark sleep, and cannot live except in his light.

So when she visits us, he comes, too. And when she sits with me, as she did today, sipping tea in her old place by the fire, he sits, too, folded improbably into a small chair near hers. At times he watches her face when she speaks, at others he turns toward me, his shoulder brushing hers, easy and familiar with her touch. At last he stands, smoothing his doublet and taking her hand. She begs for a few more minutes, pouting prettily as he pulls her toward the door.

So they are gone and my brothers have dragged themselves to bed, logy with the cakes and sweetmeats she brought. They chatter in the loft a while, like nesting birds, then settle into sleep. I tiptoe—though all the bells in Haywick could not wake that well-fed crew—to the hearth. I loosen the stone that hides the bottle, then hold the wine-colored poison to the firelight. It shimmers like an amethyst in my hand.

The fire mutters to itself and somewhere outside a dove whistles drowsily to its mate. In all the years Diamonda slept, I never

missed her as I do now. How I loathe myself for wishing she were still waiting for me beneath the glass! Should I drink to the stunted passion which prefers a caged bird to one that flies?

I open the door and carry the bottle with me to the hut. The moon is a regretful rind as I turn the key, then stand beside her old bed. Under the glass on the silk sheet is a long black shadow where she used to lie. Shall I drink to the ghost of yearning that stirs in me even now?

The casket's cover is heavier than I remember, or perhaps my trembling only makes it seem so. I put the bottle on a table, push the cover back on its hinges, and smooth her sheet with my hand. Her spot is icy cold, her warmth is somewhere else tonight. Perhaps I should drink to my six brothers, who will weep dwarf tears when they find me here.

I take off my boots and, with an old eagerness, let myself down. Instead of lying to one side, though, I take her place, my head where hers used to be, my feet straining toward the angels at the bottom of the bed. Through the open door, I see the slice of moon and hear a mouse or fox shuffle dry leaves across its path. My hand just reaches the bottle. I raise it to my lips and down it all, then close the casket's cover. Here's to the dreams that will sear my sleep when Diamonda mourns for me and presses tight against the glass.

Naked

Ride a cock horse to Coventry Cross,
to see a fine lady upon a white horse,
rings on her fingers and bells on her toes,
she shall have music wherever she goes.

They are wrong, you know. I wore no jewels when Fidelity and I rode through Coventry. The children in town still sing this song, but they are far too young to remember how it truly happened. And I am far too old to tell you a lie, close as I am to the grave. The horse was gray, not white. And the lady wore neither rings, nor cape, nor gown.

Coventry was only a small village then, and most of its families were known to me and to my lord, Leofric of Mercia. It is due to the discretion and tender feelings of those good folk, and to the love of a single child, that the nursery rhyme fails to mention the strange circumstances of my ride. The time has come, though, to strip away such lies and to let truth, as the old psalmist says, be my shield.

Leofric was wont to tell me, in those days, that I took the woes of commoners too much to heart. "You are, my precious

Godiva, inclined to weep overmuch for peasants and dumb animals, none of whom will shed a single tear for you."

"It is not with hope of return," I told him, "that I aid those less fortunate than ourselves." I remembered the eyes of the little ones when I threw coins into the streets on feast days. "It is for the sheer joy it brings me."

And, I should have added, for the absolution. It was, after all, not pleasure but forgiveness I sought the day I saddled Felicity with the stable boy's blanket instead of the silver harness to which she was accustomed. It was to erase a sin that I mounted her and rode into town without the silk and jewels by which the people knew me. And it was as a penitent that I dismounted, freighted with a secret treasure, at the small cottage where Ebba was being born.

When it was new, Coventry boasted only a single street, a long path that wound in a circle around the town, then worked its way to the river Cune on one side and to the forest of Arden on the other. The house I sought that morning was halfway around the circle, and so I was forced to pass some forty thatched huts before I reached it. Few of those poor homes had windows, but they all had doors. Soon villagers were running from one house to another, and more and more doors began to open along my way.

Some village folk came into the street to stare, others watched from their doors, and still others turned away as if it hurt to look

on me. All of them were silent, hushed by the fire in my eyes and the shock of my bare legs against the horse's sides, my naked shoulders and breasts. I was too numb with righteous anger and hurt pride to notice their expressions, to care if one was lusty or another shamed, but I remember still the old man who stepped into my path to grab hold of Felicity's bridle. He was palsied and trembling, but he held the horse fast until he had made the sign of the cross in front of my face. Then, God's work done, he fell back to let me pass.

By the time I arrived at old Ædre's house, news of my ride had already reached her. She rushed to wrap me in a rough woolen cloak before I had set both feet on the ground. "Here, my lady," she said, far more embarrassed than I. "You must not show yourself like this." She put her arms around me and helped me into the house, as if my nakedness had somehow made me infirm.

I had ridden there in the heat of passion, filled with indignation. I had not cared who stared or gawked as the horse and I made our way along. Now, with the rude cloak thrown over me, I was suddenly ashamed. I had never set foot inside any of the villagers' homes, and this one was humbler than I could ever have guessed. The floor was tamped earth, and a chicken roused itself from one corner to meet us and peck boldly at my bare toes. The room was filled with sweat and heat. Behind a blanket hung from the rafters, I heard a woman scream. She moaned, then screamed again, and I knew it must be young Fride in the pangs of birth.

I had seen her in town, a strong-limbed, laughing girl who

sold her grandmother's honey at market. Now, if the talk that had spread from town to castle, from gardener to cook, and finally to my own lady in waiting was true, this girl was giving birth to the Earl of Mercia's babe.

When yet another scream pierced us, Ædre bade me sit by the fire while she tended her granddaughter. "Aiiiiyeee," the girl wailed. And "There now," soothed Ædre. "It will not be long."

As I listened, memories filled my head and heart, memories I did not want in either place. Busying myself, I spat out the cloth bag I had hidden in my mouth. It looked like nothing, a tiny package wrapped in muslin. But when I untied the string and the square of fabric fell open on my palm, the ten gems in its center sparkled like stars.

"It hurts, Eldmoder! It hurts!" With Fride's cries, the time of my own first birth came rushing back. As I watched the shadows on the other side of the blanket, the old woman stooping to where the young one lay, I saw again the face of the midwife who had caught my daughter from the birthing chair. She'd held my babe in both hands, her forehead gleaming with sweat and her voice cracked with weariness. "There's no crying," she had said. "'Tis not a good sign."

"No, please," Fride yelled again from across the room. "Oh, no!" Though I felt little love for the girl, I could not help but smile. How young she was! How little she knew of real pain.

"See?" Ædre's voice was patient, firm. "See how it stops for a bit?" Her shadow on the blanket raised itself to a standing posi-

tion, and she sighed an old woman's sigh. "Here, now. Take some water, girl. Rest while you are able."

But still the screams went on. "Oh, by Mary's bones! I cannot take more! I cannot!"

While the girl carried on in this way, I bethought me to remove the other bag of gems I'd hidden. I reached under the cloak with which the old woman had covered me and felt inside my own body. That is how, as Fride gave birth with groans and plaints, I delivered a much smaller bundle in the wink of an eye with only two fingers.

"Aiyeee!" The wailing came again and then, abruptly, ceased.

"There she is, by the Lord's mercy." I could hear the old woman's smile in the light new cast of her voice. And I could also hear what I'd yearned for years before—the lusty, outraged squall of a newborn babe. "You've a daughter, Fride. And a long-legged lass by the looks of her."

A daughter! My knees weakened and I sank to a settle by the hearth. Beyond this bench and the table beside it, there was no furniture in the room.

I heard straw shift behind the blanket. As Fride stirred and sat up, I closed my eyes against the shadow picture I knew must come next—the babe in her mother's arms.

"Here, now, you hold her. She'll find no milk in these old teats." Ædre laughed as the babe cried, then clucked with approval as it quieted. "Ay, she's a hungry one, is she not?"

The things I did not want to remember, the hurt I'd laid to

rest, came rushing back. I saw again my little Nayla, felt the milk pressing like a flood inside me as the midwife put her to suck. What joy when her tiny mouth at last had closed round me, what despair when it opened again and all the milk spilled out.

Fride, her trials over, was laughing, cooing at her child. "Look, Eldmoder," she said. "She has small feet like yours!"

"They are all small to start," the old woman said, then soft-ened. "See how she looks at you, girl. 'Tis enough to make you fall in love up to your ears."

More rustling in the straw, more settling sounds. "And what name shall we call her, Grandmother?" the girl asked.

Ædre stood upright again, her hands on her waist. "Why, your dear mother's name, I think. Ebba is a good sound, eh?"

"Yes!" Fride bent to the little one in her lap. "You will be named for the incoming tide, little one," she whispered. "You will always come home."

How different it had been with my lost babe: I had already chosen her name, but I could not hold her gaze, nor make her take my finger in her hand. Even when I propped her against my knees and lifted her head to my face, her cloudy eyes fell away from mine.

When Ædre had made the new mother comfortable and re-turned at last to me, I pressed the jewels I had brought with me into her hands. She looked at me as though I had come to her with Moses' tablets or placed a phoenix egg in her keeping. "What be this, lady?" she asked. "What be this?" Though her

eyes could plainly tell what she held: pearls, rubies, sapphires, and an emerald as big as a walnut.

I closed her trembling fingers around the stones. "This be, good dame, your great-granddaughter's dower." As the foolish woman continued staring first at me, then at the fistful of twinkling gems, I pointed behind her to the blanket. "You surely know, as does the whole of Coventry, that the child Mistress Fride nurses not three paces from where we stand was fathered by my lord. You know, too, he may not own this babe. 'Twould not befit his title or his state to visit, to dandle her on his knee."

Once again, the dame was more embarrassed than I. She tried to throw her words, cloak-like, over this new nakedness. "You need not have come here, good madam," she said. "You need not have lowered yourself this way."

"Indeed?" I asked, again gesturing to the pair behind the blanket. "And hath not my husband already lowered himself?" Fride was barely fourteen years old and Leofric nearly forty. The girl knew nothing beyond Coventry's fields and farms; my husband was the confidant of kings and the leader of armies; armies that had laid waste whole villages, had left for dead mothers and babes.

"Men may have their way with poor lasses, madam," Ædre told me now. "'Tis the same as ever it has been. But—"

"But this shall be an end to it. These jewels will take care of the babe, better far than any father in this village could."

"We are to keep these, then?"

I was, of a sudden, angry—at the woman's thick peasant's face, at the way she continued to question her good fortune. And yes, at the picture this place had brought back: my Nayla, her lips wine-dark, her skin as white as the christening dress in which she was buried. "Do what you will with the stones," I snapped. "You may feed them to this chicken, for all I care." I stumbled over the fowl's plump body and strode to the door. "I will not come again." Leofric had been right, after all—this house, this babe, were nothing to me.

Still wrapped in the tattered garment my poor host had lent me, I set off on Felicity once more. I confess I hardly watched where I rode or cared who looked on us. The passion that had sustained me during my ride to town succumbed now to an exhaustion that overwhelmed my body and spirit. My horse walked on without my lifting the reins or digging my heels in her sides. As I yielded to an old sorrow, Felicity picked her way down the hill on which the village sat and headed toward the river Cune. I saw nothing around us, only Nayla's curled hands, her small body, the coffin fit for a doll. That tiny box had been covered over with a single shovelful of earth. In one stroke, my girl vanished, my daughter, my hope.

I already knew, then, what it was to lose everything at once. Perhaps this is why that very morning I had willingly left all I owned behind. When I told him what I planned, Leofric had refused to own the babe and bade me bring no thing of his to Fride's house.

"I shall not be part of this madness." My husband's color al-

ways rose when he was ill at ease. Now, despite his righteous words, his face and neck were all aflame. "You shall not drag me and my good name to perdition for your woman's pride."

"Forgive me, my lord," I had told him. "You mistake me. My mission in Coventry is not to punish, but to atone."

"'Mission'?" he had thundered. "'Atone'?" He followed me to my chambers, and there set his mighty frame against the door to block my way. "You sound like a very nun! Who are you to mount a mission on my behalf? To proclaim my guilt when I myself have not done so?"

"You have not denied it, sire." Nor can you, I might have added. I knew full well where he went when I turned him from my bed, when Nayla's cloud eyes haunted me and I dared not risk another babe.

"I have no need to account to gossips for my conduct."

I searched the countenance I knew as well as my own. "If not to gossips, Leofric," I asked, "then why not to your wife?"

He did not answer but, shamed, turned aside to let me pass. "Take naught of mine," he ordered as I pulled fast my chamber door. Not content with this, he pounded on the door until it shook and set to bellowing again. "Take naught of mine, I tell you. If you go, you go without my blessing or my purse."

He had thought sure to thwart me in this way, but my temper got the best of me. I opened the door when I should have bolted it, and I made a promise when I should have kept silent. "My liege," I told him, feeling my own blood rush to my face, "I will obey you in this, as in all. You have my word that I will ride

to Coventry with nothing that is yours. And because everything I have is yours, I will ride with nothing at all."

Which is how it came to pass that when I set forth a few minutes later, I left behind every stitch of clothing, every bauble and cloak my husband had ever given me. And true to my word, I took with me nothing that he owned, only what was due his child. The gems, after all, were not Leofric's. His troops had plundered them at the siege of Worcester, and he planned to make a gift of them to the church in Evesham. They were intended for God's sweet children, and, I reasoned, his new babe could surely be counted among those.

As I saddled Felicity, then, I wore only what I had been born with. And just as I knew he would, my husband chased after me, swearing oaths. "By Christ's nails!" I heard his boots against the stable door, saw the dust whirl up, tiny armies scrambling in the beam of light he had let in. "Go, then!" he said, loud enough to startle the other horses in their stalls. "Give alms where none are sought." He stepped out of Felicity's path as I backed her from her pen. "None is sought and none, I tell you, is deserved."

But if he had been full of oaths and temper when he stormed into the stable, he fell utterly silent when he saw me now. His face wore the look of someone who has walked into the path of a coiled snake, a danger with which he has not reckoned. Yet this was a danger with milk-white shoulders and breasts only half hidden by the hair that fell around me. The countenance he raised to mine reflected alarm and lust in equal measure.

I rode past him to the stable door, but still he would not, or

could not, speak. I reined the horse just outside and waited there. But my lord was paralyzed as well as dumb. He did not move, only stared and stared.

Because my mouth was stopped with jewels, I, too, must needs say nothing. A rare pair we were, then, a husband and wife with no words for each other. Just before I turned my horse, it seemed to me Leofric thought to speak. He raised one hand, and in his eyes was something like regret. But, the moment passed, he lowered his hand and I pulled Felicity's head around and rode off.

Now, as I left the village behind and the road gave way to a dusty trail, I, too, felt regret. Not for my rash rebellion that morning, or for the gift I had given old Ædre. What weighed on me like a stone, though, was the chance I had just renounced. What harm, I asked myself as I rode away from that poor hut, could it have done to hold the babe, to search for a trace of her father in her tiny face?

But I did not turn around. Hadn't I just told the old woman I would not visit again? On what pretext could I go back now? Yet as we neared the river, my arms ached for what they had not held and my eyes wept for what they had not seen. Two names chimed together in my heart: *Nayla,* with each beat of the horse's hooves. *Ebba,* with each step away from Coventry.

Felicity's nicker of surprise put an end to my pitiable musings. When she pulled short and refused to move further, I looked up

to find that the bridge by which we'd come was washed away. The river, chuckling and babbling like a child under the fallen timbers, hardly seemed strong enough to have done such damage. Perhaps thieves or villains had contrived to knock down the bridge and foil those pursuing them. Had not Leofric himself used that very trick outside of Worcester?

My horse, after her initial startle, did not seem much perturbed. She ambled to the shore and, as if she knew no harm could come from the sun-dappled stream, put down her head to drink.

There was no other way across, and I decided, too, to trust the river. "What say you, madam?" I asked her. "Do you fancy a swim in the Cune?"

Apparently she did, for when she'd finished her drink and I had got down from her back, Felicity pulled ahead impatiently. I hiked up my cloak, held her bridle fast, and the two of us started across. The water was cold, not icy, and to own the truth, I felt at first like John the Baptist or one of the old holies. Walking up to my ankles and then to my waist in the chilly stream, I pictured my violent emotions, my pride, even my intemperate weakness for corduroy and lace, being washed away.

We had not gone ten steps, though, before the water's chuckle grew to a roar. I watched branches and then a whole tree float past us. I spied a heron flying above a weedy nest caught in the stream. The bird swooped low, calling and calling to the fledglings trapped inside. When the water reached my breast and my

wet cloak threatened to pull me down, I tried to turn back the way we had come. But the current battled me so fiercely, I was forced to cling to my horse and let her carry me ahead.

The spray and the noise of the flood were fearsome, and with each step my hands nearly slipped from Felicity's broad back. But it was not until we were halfway across that I saw the goat and fully woke to the peril I was in. The old nanny, who must have thought, just as we had, to cross the stream at its narrowest point, was sailing like an ungainly bark downstream. She wore a bell that rang as she struggled against the torrent. She swept past us, bleating in chorus with the bell, and I thanked heaven for my horse's size. When the poor doomed creature's head disappeared under a swell, I closed my eyes and prayed. By the time I opened them, we had nearly gained the far bank. Then, just as we got close enough to smell the sweet woodruff in the woods beyond the shore and to touch the broken timbers of the bridge that floated past us, Felicity stumbled.

Perhaps she stepped into a hole on the river's bottom, or maybe one of the wooden beams that surrounded us knocked her off-balance. Suddenly, in less time than it takes to tell, I had lost my good horse. For as she fell, I went tumbling, too, and though I tried to grab hold of the reins and pull myself back to her side, I could not. Instead, I found myself caught up in a great rush of water that rose beneath me and then swallowed me whole.

I tasted brine and grit and watched great shadows flit past me under the brook. They may have been fish or turtles, but,

spinning and choking, I fancied they were mothers and babes, carried past me by the same current that held me in its sway. Spun round and round, in fear for my life, I mourned only two things: as I was dashed to the bottom of the stream, my hands and feet raking clots of mud, I yearned to undo the moment I had turned Felicity toward town that morning. As I prepared to die, I pictured myself pulling her short, instead, and leaning down from her saddle. I saw myself bending to Leofric, who whispered in my ear what he had wanted to tell me at the stables. "Do not go," he begged, tears in his eyes. "Do not leave me."

My other regret, the last thing I thought as the river pummeled and tossed me, was how sorry I felt that I had not kissed the baby Ebba on her forehead, had not set a tiny seal of forgiveness there—a damp print of love.

When we are most in need of His salvation, and are most repentant for our sins, the Good Lord comes to our aid. For as I felt my world grow black and my will to live snuffed out like a candle, I was suddenly pushed once more to the surface of the water. There, I grabbed one of the floating timbers, a plank that, thank Providence, was still attached to the bridge's foundation on shore. From this desperate perch, I looked out to where Felicity now scrambled in the middle of the flood. I shouted her name above the water's din, but though she thrashed and paddled furiously, without her four great legs set on its bottom she could not fight the river.

Imagine, then, my anguish as I saw my beautiful mare swept

like the nanny before her, kicking and splashing, downstream. In vain I called, in vain I reached for her tangled reins which, for a moment, danced under the current in front of me. What I retrieved from the swirling foam was only a trailing vine and, caught in its tendrils, the torn cloak in which I'd ridden here.

I cursed the water that had returned the cloak and not my faithful mare. But I dared not let go the splintered shaft of wood that bound me to land, and so was forced to watch my horse, whinnying in terror, carried away from me. I followed her course, and only when her thrashing body disappeared around the river's furthest bend did I make good my own escape.

Hand over hand, caring not for the cuts the wood gave me or for the tears that streamed down my face, I worked my way along the beam to shore. I dragged myself up the steep bank, then sat with my head in my hands and wept. I grieved for my lost horse and for my long-dead daughter. I repented, too, the rash- ness with which I had flouted my husband's will.

Though I could do nothing to bring back the dead, it was not too late, I realized with a swelling, hopeful heart, to undo the hurt I had caused the living. I resolved, wet and shivering in the shade of the forest that bordered the flood, to beg forgiveness from Leofric, to tell him how the lost babe came between us each time he sought my love. Perhaps, I thought, remembering his face in the stables, God would yet send us a healthy child. Hadn't He blessed Rebekah with twins after twenty years of barrenness? Hadn't Rachel given birth to Joseph? And Sarah to Isaac? I was

not, of course, an ancient worthy like Sarah or Rachel. I was im-
moderate and hot-tempered, but Our Savior had died for just such
as me. I rose up, my tears dried, and followed the road home.

I suppose I looked like some giant butterfly, flapping the old
cloak as I walked. The steady rhythm and the relief of the sun
on my skin soon restored my spirits. As I drew closer to the castle, I continued to make babes, not in the usual manner, of
course, but in my head. They gamboled sweetly there, already
grown old enough to romp and play with their glad parents. In
my visions, Leofric and I joined hands to race with our little
ones through meadows like the very fields I passed. When my
imaginary infants tired, or when Leofric threatened to break our
chain with his giant strides, we all fell to the ground laughing.

My cloak was dry by the time I spied the western tower and
came to the road from the stables. A lone figure on horseback approached me, and I stopped to see who it might be. As the rider
drew near, I heard a long, keening wail, a howl that set my teeth
on edge and sucked the warmth from my bones. I shivered in the
dark of that sound only a moment. For what I saw as the rider
drew nearer still is a memory that has lodged itself in my grateful
heart and which I hope to take to heaven when I die.

It was my husband, my Leofric, who came toward me, riding
a horse I never thought to see again. Felicity whinnied as she
spied me and tossed her head. Her master, though, did not glance
up but rode with his eyes closed, tears coursing down his face.

Without a saddle, his long legs hung limp, he sported neither boots nor cap. The Earl of Mercia, moaning as he rode, wore no tunic or leggings, no cloak or vest. He was naked as he was born.

"Sweet Godiva," he cried aloud, though he addressed the air, not me. "Forgive my sins. Forgive my grievous sins."

Before we lost Nayla, I had lain beside my lord. I had even found the battle scars on his shoulder and waist, had run my fingers over their toughened edges, and, yes, placed my lips there once to heal old wounds. But never had I met his body in the sunlight, seen how small and vulnerable it was against the great sky.

I ran to him and took his hands in mine. "I forgive you, my dear," I told him. "And ask only that you do the same for me."

Leofric trembled at my touch. Through his tears, he studied me as if I were a queen, an angel, Mary Herself. "I thought you drowned," he said. He slipped from the horse and knelt before me, his arms around my knees. "I thought you lost."

The sight of my husband at my feet, his pale shoulders and the small, tender bone at the base of his neck, overwhelmed me. All the fine speeches I had practiced on the way home flew out of my head.

"Do not go," he said. His voice was a whisper like the one I had heard on the river's bottom. Like a dream dreamt twice, his words, too, were the same. "Do not leave me."

"I shall not go." I placed my hand on his head and held him as if he were a babe. "I shall not go." Behind us, Felicity stamped, impatient to be off again, but we paid her no mind.

When at last my fond husband stood, it was only to hold me

again. He wrapped me in his arms and whispered more endearments. "You told me everything you have is mine," he said. "But when I thought you dead, I found that *I* had nothing left, nothing at all."

"But, sire—"

"I swore then that I would ride to church." His body had ceased trembling, and his voice grew stronger. "I would beg God's forgiveness if I could not have yours."

"You have it, good my lord."

"And I would ride as I had forced you to ride." He released me then and turned away. "Naked and alone."

I did not speak. Instead, I brought his face to mine and pressed my lips on his. No need to chatter on about my visit to Ædre, to tell how Felicity and I had come to dare the Cune. Those stories could wait. For now, we had said all that needed saying, and there was only one thing to do.

Leofric lifted me to my horse, and because he could not bear to let me go, climbed up behind me. Though she had never carried us both, Felicity set out eagerly and brought us home almost as quickly as we wished to be there. We left her in the keeping of a groom and then sped, old lovers made new, to my chambers.

I like to think that it was that very night when Ælfgar was conceived. I choose to believe that those enchanted hours, in which I learned again my husband's mysteries and he mine, were a joy that bred more joy. Nine months later, our son was born.

Like his father, Ælfgar was strong and well formed. As he grew, scenes like the ones I had imagined on my walk from the river were often played out. For he and Leofric loved to wrestle and frolic, to test each other's mettle in mock jousts or play at cock of the roost. They would sometimes include me in their capers, especially if they had need of a damsel to capture, or a keeper of scores. But there was between them a special bond, a love that springs up among men. It is not so much a secret that shuts women out as a rough-and-tumble place we cannot go.

Nor did I need more than to watch my two fine fellows at play. I had my own bond, my own sweet companion in the land of women. For, you see, I did go back to the old woman's house and to the babe who'd been born there. With my husband's permission, I visited often, and though Fride soon married and gave the girl a father, I became a sort of kindly aunt to Ebba and her family.

Like my son, Leofric's daughter grew daily more comely and blithe. Though she seldom saw the earl or her half brother, little Ebba knew no want. The jewels I had left in her great-grand-mother's care were spent on a stone house to replace their thatched hovel and a cow whose milk sold far better than honey. Before the old woman died, their state had risen so far above that of the other villagers that townsfolk took to calling them *eal-frende,* "earl's kin."

"Auntie! Auntie!" The little girl would run to meet me as soon as I stepped down from my horse. Each time she had a long list of childish triumphs and disasters to recite. "My rabbit has the

grippe," she would say, "and Father will not let me fish. I picked three apples, but no one will show me how to bake a pie."

"Well, my dear," I'd say, smiling down at her upturned face, "a witch once told me that apples are good for ailing rabbits." I would take her hand, as excited as she. "Let us see if it is true."

While I loved my son and thanked Our Savior each day for his sturdy limbs and sunny spirit, Ebba needed me more. When her mother told her no, I laughed and whispered yes. When her father thrashed her for her pranks, I slipped her trinkets and toys. In short, the child intoxicated me, and I spoiled her until she was as proud and willful as a princess.

I was not surprised, then, when, in her eighth summer, my "niece" complained that Fride had punished her for no good reason. "Mother is making me rebuild our wall," she told me, not even waiting till I had come inside. "She says I am not to kick and throw rocks at villains."

"What villains?" I asked, laughing, taking her hand in mine.

"The boys who sing the song about a lady on a horse." She frowned and stamped a dark curl out of place, so that it fell across one eye. *"Ride a cock horse to Coventry Cross . . ."* She sang in a flat, tuneless voice. *". . . to see a bare lady upon a gray horse . . ."*

Though I had never heard the ditty before, I knew its subject all too well. As Ebba sang, I saw again the crowd in the streets, the stupefied stares, the consternation.

"No mantle or dress, no gown to her name, only her hair to cover her shame." When she had finished, the girl pulled her hand from mine and pointed to a hole in the garden wall. "I took the stones

from there," she told me. "And I threw them at those rude boys until they ran away."

"I see." I let the girl lead me to the wall, where the missing stones left a gap the size of a small dog. At least ten fat stones had been pried from their nests. "And just why," I asked, "did you see fit to answer their song with kicks and volleys?"

Ebba's dark eyes narrowed and she folded her arms. "They said the song was about you, Auntie. Of course, I called them rogues and liars."

"Oh, my dear," I told her, "you must not let wagging tongues hurt you so."

"I shall not, Auntie. I made them change the song."

"Howe'er did you manage that?"

The girl smiled slyly. "Two of the scoundrels—Eadmund was one, Wilfrid, the other—came back next day to show me the bruises on their ankles." Her smile grew wider, and I doubted her mother's scolding had taken root at all. "I pledged to deal them twice the blows if they did not tell the truth. I told them your horse is white, as any fool can see." She nodded at Felicity's foal, Fidelity, who was, indeed, white, and whom I had taken to riding since her dam now saw fit to do nothing more taxing than crop grass by the stable.

"I told them, too, that you ne'er go abroad without your gowns and rings. 'My aunt is a fine lady,' I says. 'Mind ye put that in your song, or ye shall soon have black eyes as well as purple shins.'"

I could not help myself. I threw my arms around the sprite,

rewarding both her sauciness and the injuries she had done. I stooped to run my finger around the empty space in the wall. "I shall speak to your good mother," I promised. "It seems to me this lovely niche you've contrived is the very spot for the flower urn I mean to give her."

Naturally, there is more to tell, things that happened later, when both Leofric's children were grown—my husband's death, Ælfgar's victories in battle, and Ebba's marriage to a wealthy merchant. But I prefer to end my tale here, with the moment I will relive until my current affliction carries me away. While I suffer the leeches and foul-tasting medicines my physician brings me daily, while I wait for Our Holy Father to call me to him, I still take delight in remembering that girl-child. How she stamped her feet and kicked boys' shins. How she changed a song and built the world anew in the image of her love.

Thank You

Kate O'Sullivan has been, while these stories unfolded, as close as any human could come to the Ideal Editor. I laugh each time I remember her wry comments in the margins of the manuscript; I smile when I think of the cartoons, movie reviews, and other mood-lifters she sent my way; and I remain nonstop grateful for the way she "got" what I was after from the start, for the grace and tact with which she helped to grow this book.